I0823944

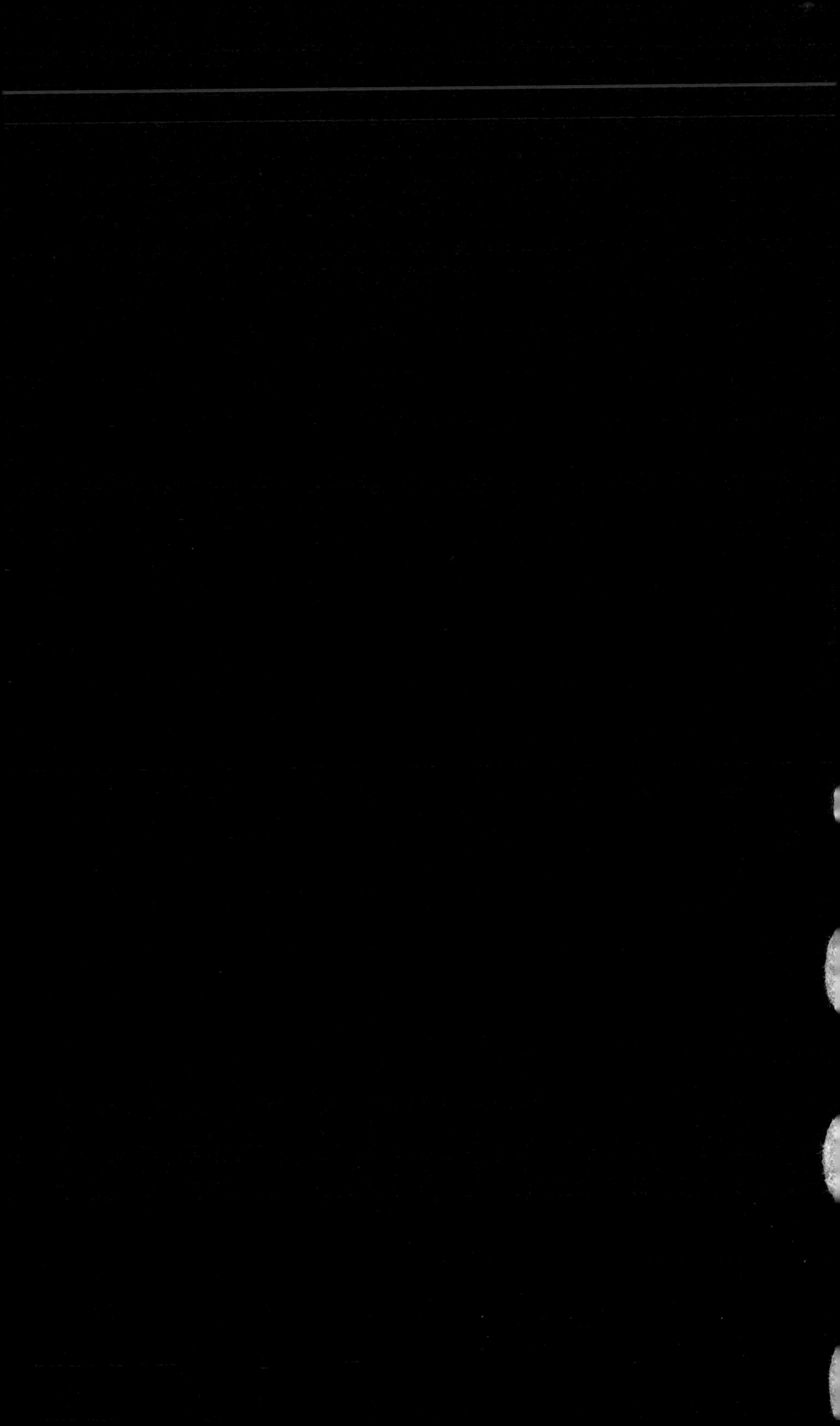

Giving Up the Ghost

Adam Lindsay Honsinger

GIVING UP THE GHOST

A Novel

Edited by Jeremy Luke Hill
Cover image by k4Orta
Book design by Jeremy Luke Hill
Set in Linux Libertine and Futura PT
Printed on Mohawk Via Felt
Printed and bound by Coach House Laid

LIBRARY AND ARCHIVES CANADA CATALOGUING IN PUBLICATION

Title: Giving up the ghost : a novel / Adam Lindsay Honsinger.
Names: Honsinger, Adam Lindsay, 1963- author
Identifiers: Canadiana (print) 20240442091 | Canadiana (ebook) 20240442105 | ISBN 9780889844810 (softcover) | ISBN 9780889844827 (PDF) | ISBN 9780889844834 (EPUB)
Subjects: LCGFT: Novels.
Classification: LCC PS8615.O505 G58 2024 | DDC C813/.6—dc23

The Porcupine's Quill gratefully acknowledges the support of the Canada Council for the Arts, the Ontario Arts Council, and the Ontario Book Publishing Tax Credit.

The Porcupine's Quill respectfully acknowledges the ancestral homelands of the Attawandaron, Anishinaabe, Haudenosaunee, and Métis Peoples, and recognizes that we are situated on Treaty 3 territory, the traditional territory of Mississaugas of the Credit First Nation.

The Porcupine's Quill also recognizes and supports the diverse persons who make up its community, regardless of race, age, culture, ability, ethnicity, nationality, gender identity and expression, sexual orientation, marital status, religious affiliation, and socioeconomic status.

The Porcupine's Quill
130 Dublin Street North
Guelph, Ontario, Canada
N1H 4N4
www.porcupinesquill.ca

Dedicated to Rain Bone

Prologue

As the sun dropped, the sky turned a deep crimson red, stalling the day's forty-degree heat down to something almost tolerable. Taking a moment in that waning light, Dhani consulted a field guide to identify a bird he spotted passing overhead. He often described the wildlife he encountered in the letters he wrote home, partly for his sister who loved animals and wanted to be a veterinarian, but also as an investigation, to be sure it was still there, the part of him that could simply look at something and appreciate the beauty in it. He had documented rabbits, porcupines, foxes, falcons, cranes, swifts, larks, several species of finch and sparrow, numerous white-rumped vultures, and a blue-cheeked bee-eater. The birds always left him wondering, if you could fly, why the fuck would you stay here?

The raptor he was watching was large and majestic, soaring west into the setting sun toward the Registan Desert. Some kind of hawk, he thought. Gold-to-black tail feathers with yellow flecks in the head area. When he matched the colour, size, and markings with a bird in the guide he scribbled down the details in his notebook: Afghan golden eagle, 9:17 pm, Kandahar, Afghanistan. He then raised his rifle and followed the rest of the bird's flight through the sight, admiring its trilling plumage, its effortless progress high above the salt cedars. As it disappeared from view he imagined it crossing the Helmand River, the Iranian border, Iraq, Syria, Lebanon, the Mediterranean Sea, Spain, Portugal, the Atlantic, and then—he lowered the rifle, let his weight pull him to the dirt, slid his arms out of his rucksack, and leaned back against the bullet-pocked wall. When he closed his eyes he was thinking of holiday dinners, his father's old jazz albums, Bollywood film festivals with his grandparents. In that moment, jacked on Rip Its, and stinking of cigarettes, sweat, and testosterone, anything and everything about home seemed iconic and precious.

Four months in, and Dhani felt like he had been away for as many years. But it wasn't just time that had been altered, his understanding of what was right and wrong had become uncertain too. His squadron had recently commandeered a residence at the edge of a village—they handed the family some cash and kicked them out. There was laundry, long dry and now dust covered, on a makeshift line in the walled courtyard that surrounded the house. Inside, a cold pot of soup sat on the stove. An intricate tapestry and a black and white portrait of a bearded man were hanging on the living room wall next to a picture of a red Lexus that had been torn out of a magazine. Candied pistachio wrappers, cigarette butts, and food scraps were scattered about the earthen floor.

Days were spent pushing through the sunbaked landscape sniffing out weapon's caches. At night they ventured out into the darkness, kicked down doors, dragged families out of their beds, blindfolded, cuffed, and hauled the men away for interrogation. These high-tension missions also involved the herding of goats, sheep, chickens, and donkeys, which they were ordered to kill. Taliban food and transportation. The dogs they shot for the hell of it.

Someone gave Dhani's boot a kick, and he jumped to his feet. The sun had completely set, but it was still hot.

"Get ready to move out."

Outside the gate of the courtyard a chorus of engines turned over. The hustle and scuff of soldiers moving in the dark.

A half hour later his section was out in the desert, the dust of the convoy rising in the star-filled sky. His guts rumbled as they made their way across eighty-seven miles of pot-holed road. At the rendezvous point, they quietly exited the armoured patrol vehicles and waited for the Afghan National Army soldiers who were lagging behind in the pickup. They surveilled the town from the cover of a stand of tamarind trees, and then, donning their night-vision goggles, they pushed in. Twenty-five yards out, the twelve soldiers paused. Someone up ahead signalled and the small group of Afghan soldiers hiked past. The noise they made as they trudged ahead seemed amplified in the darkness.

When they reached the first house, the ensuing chaos was sudden and fierce. The door was kicked open, soldiers hollering instructions, the echo of the interpreter, the terrified faces of the family they had awoken caught in the stark light of weapon-mounted flashlights. Rooms were searched; cupboards and closets were emptied. When someone smashed a glass cabinet with the butt of his weapon, one of the Afghan Army soldiers held up his hands, "No, no, bad news," he yelled. "Very religious."

The soldier who had smashed the cabinet reflexively pointed his weapon at the interpreter's chest. Without thinking, Dhani stepped between the two men. In that pungent, incense-infused moment a child sobbed in the shadows, a dog barked, and Dhani smiled. The soldier looked into Dhani's eyes. "You are one crazy motherfucker," he said. Dhani didn't realize he was holding his breath until the staff sergeant lowered his weapon. A moment later they were shoving their way through the rest of the house. Dhani felt hollow, bird-boned, light enough to take to the sky.

He awoke in the morning to find one of the old men they had dragged out of the village was lying on the floor across from him, his eyes covered with a filthy rag. A few inches from his nose was a plate of beans and rice, but of course he couldn't see it, nor could he actually eat with his hands tied. The ANA troop was huddled a few metres away around their portable cookstove. One of them held out a cigarette.

"You belong over here with us," the guy offering the cigarette said. "Your people, no respect."

Dhani couldn't say with any certainty where he belonged. He was no longer angry, scared, and fucked up like the guys and girls he rolled with. He had the sense that he was adrift now. Somewhere between the dead and the living.

After declining the cigarette, he reached into his pocket and took out the letter he had been working on. Three sheets of neatly folded foolscap filled with thoughts infected with the heat and strangeness of the desert. But now, in the wake of another adrenaline-infused night, he felt the urge to confess just how much he loved this crazy fucking rush: this mix of uncertainty and aggression, the high adrenaline spikes and the crashes, the scorching sun, its night-time equivalent of a billion tiny stars, the deep and fathomless wonder of it all. But he couldn't bring himself to finish the letter with such thoughts. Instead, the last paragraph came out as a lament, an emotional expression of something deeper, tinged as it was with longing, regret, and hope.

"It will have to do," he said aloud. He refolded the pages, slipped them into an envelope, wrote his sister's name on the front, sealed it, and tucked it into his rucksack.

Stepping out into the courtyard he waved at the captain who was sitting sentry under a beat up umbrella. The earth shimmered with the promise of another scorching day. The captain tapped a finger on his head gear. Dhani put on his helmet, took out his phone to check his messages, and then snapped three pictures of himself. He selected the one where his face wasn't blown out by the glare of the sun and sent it to his mom. Then he turned his attention to the clutch of birds that had congregated around a pile of garbage. He immediately recognized a hooded crow, several russet sparrows, and a gull. He pulled the guide out of his pocket as he approached. The birds flew off, with the exception of a single pigeon that remained amongst the debris pecking at a pop can. The sound of beak on tin reminded Dhani of the first few drops of rain on a shed roof. He watched the pigeon's determined labour until something screeched overhead. Flattening a hand over his brow, he gazed up at the clear blue sky. A golden eagle circled high on a thermal. He wondered if it was the same one that he had spotted the evening before until the intermittent tap drew his attention back to the bird in front of him. He consulted the guide and discovered that there were twelve varieties of pigeon in Afghanistan. Based on the pinkish-brown feathers and the lilac-tinged markings around its head and neck, the bird pecking at the can was a laughing dove. God is in the details, he noted. You look closely enough, and everything, no matter how common, is in some way exquisitely unique.

When he finished documenting the identification, time, and location of yet another species, he tucked the notebook and guide back into his pocket. He was just about to turn and head back inside when the IED detonated. He took the brunt of the force low on his body. Both of his legs and most of his right hand were blown off. His face and chest were riveted with shrapnel—nails, bolts, dirt, glass. What was left of him cartwheeled into the air and landed in a heap three feet away.

As the dust and debris clouded outwards, the force of the blast blew through the courtyard, out into the desert, and kept on going.

When Vanderlay called out from the front hall, the budgie in the kitchen whistled, but the house was otherwise quiet. After a double shift, which had ended in the thrum of emergency room chaos, he didn't mind coming home to an empty house. In fact, he appreciated the time to decompress, to transition back into his role of husband and father. Stepping into the kitchen, he grabbed a pen from a mug on the counter and wrote, *Happy Birthday Bailey*, on the front of the gift bag he was carrying. When his phone pinged he checked his message—*At the mall with the birthday girl, be home by 4.* He responded to the text with a thumbs-up emoji and went to the fridge. A quick snack and a cup of tea, he thought. On the bottom rack was a chocolate cake with two slices cut out of it.

He placed the cake on the table, put the kettle on, and pulled open the cutlery drawer. Among the knives, forks, and spoons was a paint-chip sampler. His wife was on one of her home improvement jags, and kitchen renovations were her latest obsession. She had been texting him about flooring, cabinetry, and paint ideas every day for the past week. A quick look around confirmed that the walls could use a fresh coat of paint, and, he noticed, there was indeed a crack in one of the Brownstone tiles under the birdcage. He recalled his wife mentioning something called *Forget-Me-Not Blue* as the colour she was leaning toward.

The moment he took a bite of cake, the budgie whistled, and then the doorbell rang. He looked over at the bird and sighed. He placed the fork down next to the paint sampler and headed to the front door.

The sun hitting the chandelier in the foyer cast shards of shifting light onto the floor and walls of the hall. By the time he got to the door he was feeling vaguely vertiginous. He took a deep breath and pulled the door open. The rich chocolate cake settled in his stomach like a stone.

The first of the two men had his hands behind his back in a state of attention. The second man, a few feet behind, had assumed a more relaxed stance with his hands in front of him, his fingers splayed across a clipboard. Vanderlay instantly recognized the posture, the formality, the subtle fluctuations in the eyes of the messenger. When he pushed the screen door open the air seemed thick and molecular.

"We're sorry to bother you Mr. Stone, but we'd like to come in and have a word, if we may."

Vanderlay resisted the impulse to slam the door closed, and took an uneasy step to his left, a position relative to the sun that reduced the soldier to a silhouette.

"Right here is fine," he said.

The soldier's reply was embedded in some kind of auditory dissonance, so Vanderlay made another adjustment to his stance and a handful of words broke through—something about bravery in the line of duty, casualty support, human remains, and then—When he heard the acronym, "IED," adrenalin and a variety of analgesic hormones flooded the limbic system of his brain and an image unfathomable and horrific took shape. The body was twisted, limbs were missing, one ragged arm reaching toward him—the manifestation of his worst fear, perfectly articulated in his son's tormented face.

When Vanderlay opened his eyes, he saw what looked like a thousand tiny explosions of light rioting above him. He extended an arm toward the ceiling, but the layers of sparkling crystals were out of reach. A slow second later he realized that he was on his back looking up at the chandelier. The two soldiers were in the hall now, staring down at him with concern on their faces.

"I'm okay," Vanderlay said as he got to his feet.

"Are you sure, Mr. Stone? You went down pretty hard."

The distortion and shock were still reverberating in the ionized air as Vanderlay straightened his back and reassured them that he was okay. "Vasovagal syncope," he said by way of explanation.

"What's that, sir?"

"I haven't slept"—he reached for the wall—"in two days."

"I'm so sorry," the soldier said, "we should have made sure you were sitting down first."

Vanderlay was looking at the two men now as if from a great distance. "It's fine," he replied. "I'd appreciate it if we could just get this over with."

The soldier with the clipboard smiled uneasily and offered some forms to Vanderlay.

"This covers funeral and burial assistance, if you need it. And this is for grief counselling—"

Vanderlay turned to the erratic chirping of the bird back in the kitchen.

"—this is my business card if you have any questions, and this is an NDF." The soldier paused as if waiting to be sure the information was sinking in.

"N-D-F?" Vanderlay said hesitantly.

"I'm sorry sir, a Notification of Death Form. I'll need you to sign here and here."

His hands were shaking as he took the pen and clipboard. Abnormal electrical activity in the thalamus, he thought.

The moment he was finished with the papers, he ushered the soldiers out the door. As they climbed into the SUV and drove away, Vanderlay's eyes were following a murmuration of starlings, drifting and shifting in a seemingly random display of collective navigation, blown to and fro it seemed, by a portentous wind.

He turned from the door, and a sharp pain spiked in his right knee. He managed to limp over to the bannister, which he used to hold himself up as he made his assessment. Possible tear in the medial or anterior ligament, he concluded.

Aiming himself at the kitchen, he took another step, this time favouring the damaged leg. "Okay," he told himself. "You got this." His laboured progress down the hall was worried by the thought that Aria and Bailey might arrive home at any minute.

By the time he got to the fridge he had a bulleted list of things to be done in his head. He pulled the freezer door open. As he grabbed a bag of ice, a whistle from Dolittle drew his attention to the window, where the bird was perched on the curtain rod. He couldn't recall opening the cage door, but there the bird was. He took a deep breath of cold air and pushed the freezer door closed. Stay focussed, he told himself. He limped back down the hall and then made his way, one slow step at a time, up the stairs to the ensuite bathroom.

He was relieved to find that the bottle of codeine—a half-finished prescription from a root canal his wife had suffered through in the spring—was still there under the sink. He took two, washed them down with a glass of water. He then eased himself onto the edge of the tub and placed the ice on his knee. As he waited for the painkillers to kick in, fragmented images flashed in the corner of his eyes—an arm, a leg, a severed hand. He felt the room vibrating around him, the air thick and undulating. Time itself, was passing with an incremental tension. While he recognized that these aberrations were symptoms of shock, he also knew that something beyond his clinical understanding had been altered.

❦

When his wife and daughter came home, Vanderlay was stirring a cup of red wine into a simmering pot of pasta sauce.

"Happy birthday," he said when they strolled into the kitchen.

Bailey gave him a hug.

"You're still up," Aria said.

Vanderlay forced a smile. "I thought I'd make my world-famous marinara sauce for the birthday girl."

Bailey looked up from the iPhone box she had just opened. "Do I smell shrimp?"

Aria shook her head at Vanderlay. "Your daughter is a vegetarian—has been for the past two months."

"Christ," Vanderlay said under his breath. "I'm sorry, Bailey."

"It's fine," Bailey said, "I'm not really hungry. We had sushi at the mall."

The bird chirped. All three of them turned to the curtain rod.

"You let Dolittle out," Aria said.

"I didn't—"

"I hate it when you do that," she interrupted. "It's always such a big deal to get him back in the cage."

"Don't worry, I'll deal with the bird," Vanderlay said. He then turned his attention to Bailey. "I got you a present, sweetheart. It's there in the bag."

Bailey looked up from her phone. "Nice wrapping job, Dad."

"Sorry, I didn't have time."

He watched her open the bag.

"An iPod?" She was clearly trying to mask disappointment.

"For your music," he said.

Aria reached for the paint sampler Vanderlay had left on the table. "Your father's living in another century," she said. "He isn't aware that everyone listens to music on their phones now."

Bailey brought her new phone to her mouth. "Siri, what is an iPod?"

As his daughter and wife laughed at the automated response, Vanderlay turned back to the stove. He couldn't think of any way to salvage the disaster, so he dropped the pot of sauce into the sink. The crash made the bird fly off into the dining room.

"It's okay, Dad," Bailey said, "I like it. It's retro."

When he turned around, Bailey and Aria were looking at him with concerned looks on their faces.

"I have bad news," he said.

"I knew something was wrong the moment I walked in the door," Aria said.

Vanderlay glanced down the hall, half expecting to see the two soldiers still standing there. "We had a visit from Repatriation Services." He looked back at his wife. Her eyes were wide, pupils fixed and dilated. Bailey was on her feet. A long moment passed, each second alive with a concussion of dread. "They say it was an improvised exploding device," Vanderlay added.

Aria was standing now, too. As his wife and daughter fell toward each other, he moved away from the counter that had been supporting his weight, and hobbled over to the table.

"He didn't suffer. He was killed instantly."

He wrapped his arms around them and felt the shock wave reverberating through the whole house, rattling windows, loosening screws, twisting studs, compromising the integrity of everything.

That evening Vanderlay took a seat in his office, and with his leg elevated and iced, he began the difficult chore of contacting friends and family. Each time he delivered the news of Dhani's death he refined the narrative until it was concise enough that he could move on without wallowing too long in the terrible pain of it. When he got to the bottom of the list, he gulped back the remains of the double martini he had been sipping. He had saved

Aria's parents for last because it was the call he was the most anxious about. Not only was his mother-in-law contending with her husband's failing memory, but their relationship with Aria had been particularly fragile since Dhani enlisted two years ago. Vanya and Annu claimed that Afghanistan was not and never had been a threat, and that the war was a "fabrication of corporate foreign interests." They went so far as to insist that their grandson never would have joined the military if he had been raised with Hindu values.

Vanderlay made the call, and after exchanging pleasantries, delivered the script to his mother-in-law. As he sat there waiting for her to absorb the news, he felt a presence in the room. He was about to turn and look behind him when his mother-in-law began to weep. He eyed the empty martini glass on his desk and lamented the fact that the gin and the vermouth were all the way downstairs in the kitchen.

When Vanya's sobbing transitioned into the incoherent articulations of a prayer, the cadence and rhythm of it lulled Vanderlay into a state of quiet contemplation. He found himself wanting to say he was sorry, but he wasn't sure why.

The prayer ended. A moment of silence passed between them.

"The question of Dhani's soul is the only thing that matters now," she said. "There are rituals that need to take place, gods that need to be solicited. This is very important."

Vanderlay was used to his in-laws' cultural perspectives—they were the reason Diwali, Pongal, and Navratri were acknowledged in tandem with Thanksgiving, Christmas, and Easter. "I understand," he said, "but we haven't gotten that far yet. We're all still—I'll talk to Aria and get back to you."

As soon as he hung up he heard the muted sound of his wife weeping on the couch in the living room downstairs. He removed the ice from his knee and pushed himself up from the chair. The swelling had gone down, but when he put his full weight on his leg he had to reach for the desk. "Christ," he said. The painkillers had clearly worn off. He took a deep breath and made his way slowly across the room and out into the dark hall. When he got to the bathroom, he heard Bailey weeping on the other side of the door. He gave a moment's thought to the grieving brochure the two soldiers had left him.

"Sweetheart," he said knocking gently.

As he stood there listening for a response, he noticed that there was a sliver of light under Dhani's bedroom door as well. He limped back down the dark hall. His hand was on the door when Bailey came out of the bathroom. "There you are," he said. "You okay?"

"I'm fine," she answered. "I just want to be left alone."

She disappeared into her room and closed the door The image of Dhani—body parts strewn about the room—flashed in Vanderlay's mind. He headed straight for the bathroom, grabbed the bottle from the drawer, and swallowed another dose of codeine.

With a freshly made double martini in hand, he headed for the living room where he found Aria staring out the window at the dark street. He made his way over to the fireplace, placed a hand on the mantle and took a sip of his drink. "I just had the strangest—"

When she turned to look at him, his wife's eyes were red and swollen. "What are we going to do?" she said.

The question left him feeling completely out of his depths. "I don't know," he answered stupidly. "Whatever it takes." He put his drink down and hobbled across the floor. When he took her in his arms, the bird flew in from the hall, circled the room twice, and then thudded into the window.

"What was that?" Aria said.

"The bird's still out," Vanderlay answered.

He checked behind the couch where the bird had fallen and was relieved to find Dolittle appeared to be okay. A moment later he was in the air again, and after another frantic circle of the room he flew out into the hall.

Aria turned back to the window. "I can't shake the feeling that there's been some kind of a mistake."

"What do you mean?" Vanderlay said.

"I mean, what if there's been a mix up. I don't know, an administrative error? What if there's more than one Dhani Stone in the forces?"

"Sweetheart," he said. He waited until she turned to face him again. "Our son is—"

"I just think we need to be sure," she said. "Double-check."

Vanderlay felt the same presence in the room that he had sensed upstairs.

When she turned back to the window, he made his way to the fireplace to retrieve his martini. "I'll make some calls in the morning," he said.

❧

Over the next few days Aria returned to the couch where she sat in her housecoat looking out the front window, Bailey stayed in her room, emerging only to use the bathroom or to forage for snacks. Vanderlay, on the other hand, kept himself busy: paying bills, making grocery runs, and preparing meals. While these activities provided him with a much needed sense of purpose, the inexplicable weirdness continued. As he limped his way throughout the house he had the sense that someone had just left each room that he entered—lights were left on, drawers and cupboards were open. Either these aberrations were the residual symptoms of shock, he reasoned, or the result of the fact that he'd been mixing opioids with the occasional martini.

On the day the codeine ran out, he drove to the hospital to have his knee looked at. A colleague confirmed a Grade II medial collateral ligament tear. Physiotherapy and rest were recommended. In the meantime, he was given a pair of crutches and a prescription for the pain.

Aria was waiting for him in the front hall when he got home. He was surprised but relieved to see her dressed and on her feet.

"I thought I noticed you limping," she said. "What happened?"

He leaned the crutches against the wall. "I somehow sprained my MCL, but I'm fine." He pulled a bottle of pills out of his pocket and gave it a little shake. "Just need to take it easy."

"OxyContin? That's a bit strong isn't it?"

"It's take only as needed," he said, as if that was an answer to the question.

Aria took his jacket. "I cooked—you hungry?"

"I am," he said.

He followed her into the kitchen where Aria went to the stove and pulled out a glass dish.

"I don't mean to rush things," Vanderlay said as he took a seat, "but we have to talk about what's next."

She put a plate of food down in front of him and stepped back to lean herself against the counter. "I'm sorry," she said. "I realize how crazy it sounds, but I can't stop thinking that if we just give it a little more time Dhani will, I don't know, it feels like having a funeral would mean we have given up on him somehow."

He looked down at the plate—the asparagus, the rice, and the chicken breast—at the glaring whiteness of space between each item. "According to the literature, one of the stages of grieving is *denial*," he said. "It's quite normal—"

She was crying again.

It's all a matter of physics, he thought. An explosion creates a rapidly expanding force that pushes the atmosphere away from its central point. This wave is followed by an equal force rushing back in to fill the vacuum created by the initial explosion, which creates a secondary shock. "If you need more time," he added, "that's okay. We'll figure it out."

Aria slept on the couch that night. Her sobbing, which Vanderlay could hear through the vents, was interrupted now and again by the sound of footsteps in the hall. At one point, as he was laying there in the dark, he felt the presence of his son so acutely that he was sure he was there in the room with him. He knew there was no empirical evidence to support the existence of ghosts, and yet—

In the morning he limped into the kitchen to find Bailey eating cereal from the box. When he greeted her, she offered him a smile, but she didn't say anything.

"I was thinking of making bacon and eggs for breakfast," he said as he opened the fridge. "How does that sound?"

She placed the cereal box on the table and pushed it away from her. "Thanks, but I'm still a vegetarian, Dad."

"I'm sorry," he said. He poked around for an alternative. "What about French toast?"

When he turned from the fridge with a carton of eggs in his hand she got up and left the room.

"Christ," he said.

Aria walked into the kitchen as he was steaming the milk for an espresso. He handed her the coffee when it was done. "I'm worried about Bailey. She hasn't said more than three words to me since—" He pushed the fridge door closed. "I swear I just closed that."

"She's okay," Aria said, "I had a good talk with her last night."

Vanderlay was aware of how acutely numb he was feeling. How the pain was very much there, mangled, tortured, and unbearable, and yet, it was all a few layers below the need to get through each daily task.

"I've been thinking about the funeral," Aria said. She placed her coffee on the counter and looked to the window. "I'd like to keep it small and simple, just a reception of close friends and family." When she turned to face him, her expression was sad and pained all at once. "But on the condition that there's no religious stuff."

The first thing that came to Vanderlay's mind was his in-laws. "What about—"

"Don't worry about my parents," she said, "I'll deal with them." The bird flew into the room and landed on the top of the cage. "In fact, I'll call them right now."

Vanderlay reached into the pocket of his bathrobe and took out the bottle of painkillers. He placed a pill in his mouth and drank what was left of Aria's abandoned coffee.

The reception five days later was held in the backyard. The latticed arbour resplendent with morning glory was flanked by two tables—a photo of Dhani and a guestbook on one, a pewter urn and a large vase of gladiolas on the other. The catering involved two meat and two vegetarian dishes, an open bar, a cook, and a server.

Vanderlay was watching his mother-in-law insert a stick of incense into the soil of a terracotta pot when something drew his attention to the sliding doors. The image in the reflection of the glass was only there for a second, but it was enough to unsettle him. He had caught a fleeting glimpses of his son once in the dark hallway outside the bedroom and again that very morning in the bathroom mirror while he was brushing his teeth. These hallucinations, paired with the crutch he had been using to get around, had left him feeling vulnerable and exhausted.

When his father-in-law stepped up to the podium to start the ceremony, Vanderlay's mind turned to this newest worry. His wife had relented to the idea of her father delivering the eulogy, but she had made Vanderlay promise to intervene if the speech become dogmatic or otherwise religiously prescriptive.

Annu cleared his throat, and a hush made its way across the yard. The metallic clang of a lid being closed by the caterer, who had just given the sweet potato agnolotti a quick stir, was followed by the bark of a dog several yards over. For a moment it looked like Annu was trying to figure out where he was and who all these people were, but when the smoke of the burning frankincense made its way to the podium, his eyes cleared, and he withdrew a neatly folded piece of paper from his pocket.

As he began his speech, Vanderlay reached into his own jacket, uncapped the prescription bottle and discreetly swallowed an extra Oxycodone for good measure.

Annu read the first few sentences in Hindi and then paused to take off his glasses. "My apologies," he said, "I forget sometimes that we are all English speakers here—"

A lawnmower started up in a neighbouring yard. He waited for the machine and the god-awful noise it was making to pass along the back fence, and something drew his attention into the sky. During this awkward pause it became apparent to all that Annu had once again lost his bearings.

Vanya appeared at Annu's side, folded the piece of paper containing his speech, and tucked it into the pallu of her white sari. "Please excuse my dear husband," she said, "as you can all imagine, this is a very trying time for us. Not only have we lost our grandson, but we have conceded to a number of compromises regarding the traditions of our culture." She paused and set her eyes on her daughter. "It is our belief that after death the Atma is released from the mortal frame, and without prayer, ritual, and the proper proceedings, the released Atma will remain, like a ghost, in limbo. In other words, Dhani's soul will not be able to transmigrate until the proper ceremonies are administered—"

Vanderlay was pondering the idea that the hallucinations that he had been having might actually be Dhani's ghost, when he felt Aria place her hand on his arm. It took him a moment to realize that the pressure she was inflicting was his cue to get up and intervene. But things were moving slowly now. The pharmaceuticals were at work on his brainstem and spinal cord. When he heard Vanya declare that Dhani's death was the result of karmic forces, Vanderlay understood why his wife had placed a moratorium on any religious references in the eulogy.

The moment he was on his feet he knew he was in trouble. He steadied himself and focussed on Vanya, who was now reading from a marked section of the Bhagavad Gita. He took a few tentative steps forward, but there seemed to be a delay between what his mind was thinking and what his body was doing. By the time he arrived at the podium, Vanya was closing the book.

"It is customary in our culture," she said, "when there are concerns regarding the welfare of the soul of the deceased, that on the one year anniversary of the death, a sraddha must be performed. Without the Tarpana, Dhani will remain a wandering ghost, and we, his family will be destined to suffer the malefic effects of his demise." She then took Annu by the arm and led him back to their seats.

Vanderlay, who was now alone at the podium, stood there for several uncomfortable seconds looking out at the faces seated in front of him: relatives, friends—some of whom he did not recognize. The moment he focussed on his daughter, he saw the distress in her eyes. This is all going horribly wrong, he thought. He then turned to the empty chair where his wife had been sitting. He scanned the yard until he spotted her at the catering table gulping back a glass of chardonnay. He knew at that moment that he had failed his whole family: his in-laws, his wife, his daughter, and his son.

As he breathed in the heady smell of the incense, his injured knee began to spasm. His eyes went to his cane, which he had left leaning against his seat. This is it, he thought, the compression of the blast that had collapsed back in on itself had caused yet another shock wave.

He adjusted his weight to the side of his uninjured leg, and for a moment it seemed like he may be all right. But then his good knee started to tremble, and he felt himself timber once again. When he went down, he took the memorial table and everything on it with him.

He was immediately aware of the strangely comforting softness of the ground. Part of him wanted to just lie back and rest there in the grass, take a break from the whole convoluted mess. But then he felt the dampness soaking into the knees of his pants, and he noticed the vase of flowers lying on the ground next to him.

He was trying to get to his feet when he saw Bailey bend with a horrified look on her face to pick up the urn, the contents of which had spilt onto the grass. There was nothing else to be done so he returned to his knees and helped his daughter, pinch by pinch, put the charred grit back into the vessel.

363 days after Dhani's death

The passing of time reverberates, tumbles and stumbles, sometimes in painful increments, and sometimes in large vacant swaths of numbness. The shadows creep across the walls, stealing hours out of each evening to shroud the world in a deep grey fog. Driveways of parked cars, grass brittle and brown, trees on the boulevard sentient under a bleak sky, dropping gold and red leaves with their own kind of indifference. It was as if the pain and the weather were conspiring, a mirror to the thoughts and feelings weighing so heavily on your heart. And this remoteness, born without complaint or resistance turned the very air into something sluggish, foreign to your lungs. As the equinox came and went, worrying trenches were stomped into the earth. Patterns of routine and sorrow, a map of sorts, declaring, despite the passing of time, that the world had become a counterfeit version of normal, a cheap rip off with its scorched edges, its divots and potholes. Every thought, coloured by the sepia, not of nostalgia, but of absence. You wake up to find yourself leaning over a bowl of cereal, the spoon halfway to your mouth, wondering how it is that you got there. The past, the moments before, as unknowable as the moments to come. You are stuck, so it seems, in this drift in and out of awareness, all the while the distant sound of a striking hammer, dull blows of metal on rock, emanating from somewhere just over the rise.

One

In the year following the funeral, Vanderlay's hallucinations grew more frequent, and Bailey and Aria grew more distant and unpredictable. When the three of them were in the same room, their collective grief made Dhani's absence seem palpable. Aria kept referring to Dhani as if it was just a matter of time before he walked in the door, and Bailey was so on edge that a simple good morning could be interpreted as an affront toward her own ineffable sorrow.

Staying busy had always been Vanderlay's way of dealing with stress, and the extra shifts he took in the understaffed triage only made things worse. Before long he was napping in the staff room, in the car in the hospital parking lot, whenever he had a moment off his feet. By the time Bailey moved out in the spring, he was moving through the world single-mindedly, numb, and distracted. It was in this half-awake state that he noticed a box of books sitting at the foot of the stairs, and then an empty space on the wall where a Klimt lithograph once hung. He assumed Aria was doing some spring cleaning and left it at that. But then a week later, he came home to discover a moving truck in the driveway. Inside he found Aria in the living room wrapping newsprint around one of the tribal masks that she had purchased on a trip to Madagascar. As soon as she looked up at him, he knew she was leaving him. He loosened his tie—he needed to breathe, to make room for the possibility of reason. "Aria, please don't do this," he said.

She placed the wrapped mask in a box, folded the flaps and sealed it with a strip of tape. Vanderlay stepped forward to let two men carrying the sofa pass.

"I'm really sorry," she said. "I just can't explain it. I mean, I'm not really sure what I'm doing, but I just can't sit here waiting anymore. I need to get out of this house, or I'll go crazy."

His mind went to the pills in his pocket, to the bottle of gin in his office upstairs. "All the literature says that the first year is the hardest," he said. "We just have to hold it together, and we'll get through this."

"Jesus, Vanderlay. What do you know about grieving? All you do is work. You're not even here when you're here—" She looked at him with tear-filled eyes. "Have you cried, even once?"

He looked down at his shaking hands. "It's an occupational hazard," he responded. "Years of treating gunshot wounds, suicide attempts, and other ER trauma have limited my lacrimal system to the production of basal and reflexive functions only."

Aria shook her head. "You've got a rational explanation for everything—" Her attention shifted suddenly to a mover who had just thrown a heavy blanket over the dining room table. "Careful with that," she said, "it's a Thos. Moser." She looked back at him. "What was I saying?" she asked.

"You're leaving me."

She sighed and wrote "Artifacts" across the box with a marker, "I'm sorry," she said. "I really am."

Later, alone in the kitchen, Vanderlay found himself considering each beat of his heart, the atria and ventricles, the pulmonary and aortic valves, the sinoatrial node transmitting electrical signals to the upper and lower chambers. He grabbed a chef's knife and pressed the tip against his sternum. He imagined making an incision, removing his trauma-scarred heart and replacing it with a new and undamaged organ. Maybe then, he thought, I might be able to produce a single drop of H_2O, sodium chloride, mucus, and lysozyme. One goddamn tear.

Reverberations from the explosion continued, and as Vanderlay withdrew further into his own despair, the time between shifts became unbearable. Alone in the empty house, the hallucinations worsened, and the flying dreams that inevitably left him acutely aware of the weight of his own body, plagued his sleep. To compensate, he had adopted a daily regimen of pharmaceuticals: opiates to alleviate moments of dire emotional stress, sedatives to help him sleep, and stimulants to get him back on his feet. Work was the only place where he had any sense of agency and purpose. It was a world where the enemy could be diagnosed and attacked with an orchestrated aggression.

And thus the months went by until, three days before the anniversary of his son's death, Vanderlay awoke on the dining room floor. The angled light coming through the sliding doors stretched all the way to the far wall. Late afternoon, he guessed. His attention went to the ache pulsing in the occipital region of his skull. When he was aware enough to notice the half-empty bottle of Scotch and the futon he was lying on, it all began to make sense.

Both the whisky and the mattress were gifts delivered earlier that day by his colleague, Dr. Takeru Shin. Though Takeru had claimed that the futon was an old spare, Vanderlay could tell as they struggled to get it through the front door, that it was in fact brand new.

"I'm glad it can be of some use," Takeru had said as he dropped his end on the floor, "until you get a proper bed." He then turned in a slow circle surveying the empty room. "Jesus, Vanderlay, Aria really did take everything."

Vanderlay was used to the look of concern in his friend's eyes. On the occasions he found himself at some social function or other, people would turn on a light or open the curtains when he entered the room as if his presence darkened every doorway he passed through. He learned to respond with levity or humour whenever it could be mustered. "Not quite everything," he said, "she did leave the lawnmower and my golf clubs." As he took a swing with an invisible driver, a whistle from the kitchen broke his concentration, and the ball sliced into the rough. "And the budgie," he added. "She also left Dolittle."

Takeru's gaze came to rest on a pile of dirty plates in the corner. "How long have you been living like this?"

The mention of time reminded Vanderlay that the sraddha was now days away. He moved as if the force of something had just shoved him toward the kitchen. "I don't know how long it's been," he said as casually as possible. "Aria took the calendar too."

Takeru picked up his briefcase and followed. "You're living in and empty shell," he said, "—nothing but lumber, drywall, and brick—a house, not a home."

Vanderlay wasn't sure why he couldn't tell his friend that he had no intention of buying a new bed. Nor could he bring himself to mention the flying dreams and the discomfort that had taken up residence in his gut.

He stopped at the sink and pulled the curtains open.

"The truth is," he said, "this house isn't empty at all. Each and every room is a cluttered mess of memories and emotions." He looked up at the clear blue sky. "In fact," he added, "I'm pretty sure this house is haunted."

Takeru looked around the kitchen. There was no table or chairs, so he placed his briefcase on the counter. "Some people say the dead don't rest until those that mourn them let them go."

Vanderlay pulled the window open and took a deep breath of fresh air. "The in-laws are holding a sraddha on Sunday," he said. "Whether that actually helps or not, I don't know, but at least we'll all be together again."

Takeru opened the latches of his briefcase.

Vanderlay smiled when he saw the bottle in his friend's hand. "I'm more of a martini man," he said, "but I wouldn't say no to a dram of Lagavulin. The question is," he turned to the cupboard beside him, "do I have a couple of glasses worthy of such a fine single malt?" He pulled open the cupboard doors and then nodded toward the cabinet above the stove. "Check those."

"No furniture is one thing," Takeru said, scanning the empty shelves, "but no whisky glasses is simply inexcusable. You really need to get your shit together."

Vanderlay opened the cupboard next to the fridge. It too was empty except for the paint sampler sitting on the bottom shelf. His eyes went to the birdcage and then to the front door. He waited a second for the sound of the two soldier's ringing the bell. "Déjà vu," he said quietly.

"What's that?" Takeru asked.

Vanderlay felt a twisting sensation in his gut. "Nothing," he said, "it's just a bit of indigestion."

Takeru uncorked the Scotch and held it for a second to his nose. "Seriously," he said, "I'm worried about you. When's the last time you took a holiday?"

Vanderlay went to the dishwasher and pulled out two mugs. "That, my friend," he said as he handed Takeru the least dirty of the two, "is exactly what my wife used to say."

Takeru poured himself a modest shot and then handed the bottle to Vanderlay, who poured a larger one. They toasted and drank, and as each minute passed, Vanderlay was relieved that Takeru didn't mention the pile of mail sitting unopened on top of the stove. He didn't say a word about the empty Styrofoam containers and pizza boxes, or the plastic cutlery, or the bottle of alprazolam on the counter. Both men ignored the echo of their voices reverberating down the hall, which gave the impression that there was another pair of men having the same conversation a second or two later on the landing at the top of the stairs. Instead, they just stood there in the kitchen sipping Scotch, talking of pitching wedges, subdural hematomas, the peaty nuances of Islay malts, anything and everything except the emptiness around them.

By the time Takeru picked up his briefcase and headed to the door, the uneasiness in Vanderlay's stomach had been nullified by six ounces of 16-year-old, heavily peated, Lochan Sholum malt. Tired and inebriated, he stumbled into the dining room and collapsed on the futon where he dreamed that he was soaring over a quilted landscape toward a deep, dark body of water.

Slightly disoriented from the flying dream, he got to his feet, steadied himself against a tinge of vertigo, and then glanced at his watch. He'd been out for about two hours. "Coffee," he said aloud.

When he got to the kitchen he stared at the spot where the espresso machine used to sit. He then put the kettle on and went over to the cage. Dolittle bobbed on his perch and pecked a few times at Vanderlay's arm as he reached for the yellow plastic trough of water. The damn thing had a sharp beak, which, he guessed, was why is wife hadn't taken it with her.

After filling the water trough, he closed the wire door and stood there thinking about what Takeru had said earlier about a holiday. The only time he had really taken time off work was the four days he'd missed when Dhani died. Otherwise, he'd worked through a bout of streptococcal pharyngitis, chronic stomach pain, and lately, a number of hangovers.

He went to the sink, dumped a spoonful of coffee into a mug and then grabbed the kettle. As he poured the water, the late afternoon light illuminated the mess cluttering the countertop. Maybe Takeru is right, he thought. Maybe it is time to get my shit together. A few seconds later he was in the dining room, where he took a second to survey the random things scattered on the floor: the crumpled blanket, the folded towel he had been using as a pillow, the newspapers, the socks, the bottle of Scotch, the dirty dishes in the corner.

Back in the kitchen, he piled the plates, coffee cups, and cutlery he was carrying into the sink, stuffed all the empty takeaway containers into a garbage bag, poured a shot of whisky into his coffee, and grabbed the broom. After he swept out each room, he gathered the takeaway containers and empty bottles. He eventually had to load all the smaller garbages into one large bag and then drag everything out to the bins in the garage. As soon as he was inside again he poured another shot into his mug and went back to work. Before long, a large load of towels and clothes were tumbling in the washer. He then cleaned the tub and the toilet, ran the dishwasher, wiped down the counters, disinfected the fridge.

Once the house was in order he grabbed a pen and paper. He had just added whisky glasses to the shopping list when he noticed Dolittle was out of his cage again. He followed the sound of the bird into the living room. When he located him on windowsill pecking at the glass, Vanderlay placed a hand on the fireplace mantle to steady himself. As he waited for the crucial moment to pass, he saw through the window, a dark grey line of clouds converging on the horizon.

Aria's apartment, an 800-square-foot studio featuring exposed brick, ductwork, and the constant hubbub emanating from the walls of the neighbouring units, was not the fortress of solitude she had anticipated when she moved out. Not only was the building poorly insulated, but it was full of millennials, whose presence so compromised the bohemian charm she had envisioned that she never really settled in. Three months had passed, and most of her things were still piled in the middle of the studio where the movers had left them. The result was a cluttered maze of unopened boxes and furniture. She had to squeeze between the buffet and hutch and the eighteenth-century French armoire to get at her dresser, the lower two drawers of which were blocked by a weighty Camphor trunk. The dining room table had a blanket draped over it, on top of which sat several boxes with things like *pottery, sculptures, books*, and *photographs*, markered across the front. A chandelier covered the smoked-glass top of a coffee table. The silk Damask upholstered sofa was occupied by a stack of teakwood crates filled with classical music LPs. Three framed lithographs—a Klimt, a Miró, and a Kandinsky, were leaning against the armrest. The only real usable floorspace was in the open concept kitchen where she was presently sitting on a stool bowing the first movement of Beethoven's String Quartet No. 13.

She hadn't touched the violin since she quit her position at the TSO twenty years ago, and reacquainting herself with the instrument was proving to be rife with frustration. While she was pleased to find that she could still intuit her way along the neck, when it came to certain bow techniques, her elbow and wrist felt like rusted hinges.

She was just beginning to feel a degree of grace returning to her stroke when her phone rang. The moment she saw her husband's name on the screen she placed the violin on the counter and accepted the call.

"Hi," he said, "do you have a minute?"

"I'm in the middle of something, but go ahead."

"I wanted to ask if you—"

When he didn't finish the question, Aria began to feel a little anxious. "What is it?" she said. "Is everything okay?"

"Everything is fine. I was just wondering—do you put the fabric-softener in at the beginning or at some other point in the cycle."

"Laundry," she said, "I haven't heard from you in two weeks, and that's what's on your mind?"

"I just did a load, and the towels aren't as soft as when you wash them. I thought I must be doing something wrong."

"Everything you need to know," she said, "is in the directions written on the container—"

"The truth is," he interrupted, "I'm calling because I miss you. I want you to come home."

Aria took a deep breath. At some point the idea of returning home had become synonymous with giving up, which in her mind meant her son's passing had become peripheral somehow.

"If you don't have time right now," he said, "maybe we can talk about it on Sunday at the ceremony."

She lowered the phone and stared at the red button on the bottom of the screen. She hadn't told anyone that she wasn't going to the sraddha—that the approaching anniversary of Dhani's death had become a sort of deadline for all the confusing things she was grappling with. Most of which were born out of the crazy idea that her son might still be alive, a notion that her therapist assured her was a natural part of the grieving process and that it would, in time, give way to a stage of acceptance. But the feeling did not dissipate; in fact, it had grown so strong that she found herself walking out of a travel agency last month with a ticket to Kabul in her hand.

"Aria?"

Her eyes settled on the machine sitting on her countertop, and as she took inventory of the copper globe, the brass attenuator, the resonating disc, the harmonic scale ring, and all its other peculiar metallic bits, she wiped at her tearing eyes. The easiest way to re-establish control, she thought, was to change the subject. "Have you heard from Bailey?"

"I haven't," he said. "She won't return my calls."

"It's her birthday on Monday."

"I know. I got her a present. Which reminds me, do kids still use headphones?"

"She's not technically a kid anymore, but yes, I think she'd like that."

A moment passed, during which the stress seemed to evaporate between them, but then her mind returned to the music.

"I really have to go," she said. "I promise I'll call you later."

As Aria picked up the violin, she was thinking about her ill-fated trip and the surreal encounter she had in the Registan Desert. The sunbaked plains, the nine-hour bus ride, the bribes at the roadblocks, the fourteen kilometre trek on the back of a mule to the village where Dhani was reportedly killed. The disappointment of finding the place abandoned—nothing but a couple of decrepit chickens remained. She had wandered through the narrow streets past bullet-pocked walls, the eerie emptiness disturbed now and again by something rattling in the breeze. Overwhelmed by the staggering presence of the idea that her son might actually be gone forever, she pointed herself toward the setting sun and headed out into the desert. A couple kilometres into her aimless wandering she saw what looked like an eagle soaring in the sky. It had just disappeared into the blinding sun, when her skin began to tingle. A moment later there were tiny sparks of electricity pinging in the air. All at once she felt weightless, suspended, or so it seemed, in a gentle embrace. It was so strangely comforting that she wondered if she had died and entered a state of cessation—what her mother would have called one of Brahman's macrocosms. In this protracted moment she heard music: Beethoven, Bach, Mozart... Each composition sounded like it was being played on an old phonograph. By the time the sixth composition was coming to a close, she had the sense that the sequence was curated to convey some kind of a message, but then, a beat into the first note of the seventh composition, the transmission ended.

She woke up disoriented in a hospital in Kandahar with a strange diagram in her head. The doctors explained it away as "delusional hysteria," a condition brought on by exposure, isotonic dehydration, and a slur of acronyms symptomatic of being lost in a desert for two days. When she returned home, Bailey and Vanderlay were at the airport waiting for her. "I'm sorry," she kept saying. "Sorry for making you worry. Sorry for acting so crazy." But she wasn't. What everyone was calling a breakdown, in her mind, was an otherworldly transcendental experience.

After a couple weeks of rest and therapy she opened her laptop and began searching for information that might make sense of what had happened. Her investigations led to the works of John Worrell Keely, a nineteenth-century inventor who had built a series of strange and beautiful machines that were activated by notes played on a *sympathetically harmonized* musical instrument. Keely's work made her realize that the mysterious diagram was actually a blueprint. After several visits to the hardware store, the junkyard, and a local pawnshop, she managed to assemble a crude machine of her own. The next day she was on a stool pulling her old violin down from a closet shelf. She began working under the hypothesis that if she played the first six compositions over and over, the interrupted seventh piece would reveal itself. What this would accomplish she didn't know, but she was certain that it had something to do with the unfathomable pain in her heart.

When she started playing again, her rusty technique and the shortcomings of the violin itself triggered a violent impulse that had recently led to the destruction of two other instruments. The first, a cherished Heinrich Roth given to her by her father when she graduated from the Royal Conservatory, was slammed against the fridge three weeks ago. The second, a brand new Ren Wei Shi with an unforgivable hint of unevenness higher up the neck, was destroyed underfoot a week later.

Before she could stop herself, she heaved the violin she was currently playing at the wall. It exploded against the brick and fell to the floor. She turned away from the splintered mess and rolled up her sleeve. On the inside of her arm was a list:

Find 7th composition
Therapist 4pm
Oliver Silverman 2037 Queen W. 7pm

She looked at the clock, grabbed a pen and added the words, *Buy new violin.*

In the months after the funeral, Bailey had grown so despondent that she could barely muster the will to get up each morning. The question, *what's the use if everything is going to die?* seemed to overshadow everything. At some point she began to apply the bare minimum: she brushed her teeth, but she didn't bother to floss; she washed her hair, but no longer used conditioner; and by the last semester of the school year, not only had she skipped enough classes that she was no longer sure her GPA was high enough, but nothing seemed more pointless than a post secondary degree. This malaise was occasionally punctuated with rash decisions that often led to dramatic outcomes. The tattoo of Kali, the goddess of death, whose blue face took up the length of her arm from elbow to wrist, was bad enough, but accosting her mother in the front hall and telling her she was moving out was the most regrettable by far.

"Oh, Bailey," her mother had replied. "Really? Now? I'm already late for my therapist appointment."

Bailey shrugged, knowing full well how much displays of indifference annoyed her parents.

"We'll talk about this tonight," her mother said as she slid her arms into her jacket.

"Talk?" she replied. "I don't think there's anything to talk about. I'm old enough to decide for myself."

Her mother paused with her hand on the door. "You're breaking my heart. Do you know that?"

"You're not the only one with feelings around here."

The taxi honked outside.

"Okay," her mother said, "I don't want to fight with you, but if you move out, you'll need to pay your own way—like the adult you seem to think you are."

Her mother stepped out the door, but it didn't feel like a victory. Bailey was disappointed by how easy it had been.

With no choice but to follow through, she got a job at the mall offering perfume samples to shoppers who walked by the Chanel booth, but she was dismissed after a few shifts for spending too much time texting while on the floor. She was terminated from a second job selling cruelty-free beauty products for failing to meet her sales quotas. She then answered an ad for a part-time position at Venus Envy, *a purveyor of adult marital aids*. While there was a degree of satisfaction in just how much this would genuinely dismay her parents, the job was a bit of an embarrassment for her too. When her roommate bailed on her and left her with the lease, she discovered that being an adult—working, paying rent, and eating as much sushi as she wanted—wasn't doing anything to shift the sense of pointlessness that greeted her each morning.

When her mother had called with the news that she was moving out, Bailey fell back on the couch and squeezed Felix, her threadbare stuffed dog, to her chest.

"I know this must be hard for you," she added, "but I can't stay in this house either."

In that moment, Bailey's own anxieties were eclipsed by a new and equally troubling worry. She tightened her grip on Felix and asked the question, "Are you getting divorced?"

"I love your father," her mother said, "but it's complicated, you know, this year has been hard on all of us. So the answer to your question is—no. I don't know. We'll see."

Bailey felt her apartment tilt. When she closed her eyes, the couch she was sitting on began to slide toward the door, down the stairs, and then along the street, until three and a half blocks later, she found herself in the office of a Gestalt-based psychotherapist who also dabbled in career counselling.

She took the little pencil and the assessment form that the receptionist handed her, forced herself to circle the numbers on each sliding scale. She was certain that this exercise amounted to little more than a useless administrative attempt to get inside her head, but the office had free wifi, so she decided to wait for the results.

By the time the counsellor invited her into her office, Bailey was feeling a bit better—she had just clicked the *Buy Now* button on a Stitch Sketch OtterBox for her phone.

After offering Bailey a seat, the counsellor put on a pair of reading glasses. "Your assessment points to anxiety, low-grade depression, and some anger management issues"

Bailey turned off her phone but she didn't put it away. "You can add low self-esteem to that list if the idea is to point out all my flaws. But I don't think I'm depressed, I'm just hopelessly miserable. I mean, it's not depression if there's a valid reason for your sadness, is it?"

The counsellor leaned forward, jotted something down on a piece of paper, and then sat back again. "What's making you sad?" she said.

"I don't know, climate change, our imperilled democracy, the fact that life basically amounts to the daily management of a never-ending series of disappointments."

"Those are serious problems for sure. How are things at home?"

Before she could stop herself she admitted that she was in fact supposed to be studying veterinarian medicine, but that it had recently dawned on her that this occupation, more often than not, involved the euthanization of aged and diseased family pets. "I always wanted to help animals," she added, "not kill them."

When the counsellor told her that the animal shelter down the road was hiring, Bailey hurried home, put on her Jane Goodall tee-shirt, went to the shelter and asked to speak to the manager.

An hour later she was filling out the requisite forms to begin her internship as a dedicated Paw-tner at the SPCA.

She had only been working at the shelter for two days when she adopted Bruno and Charlie, a pair of calico guinea pigs. They were from the same litter, and so in her mind they couldn't be separated. Three days later she brought home the painted turtles, Raphael and Leonardo. Tulip and Hugo, the two sable point Mini Rex rabbits, weren't technically related, but they had been cohabiting in the same box for several weeks and so, once again, Bailey couldn't adopt just one. Before she knew it, she had become what, Jill, her manager, referred to as a rescuer, a term used to describe clients who become addicted to the act of saving the abandoned and abused wards of the shelter. She was so caught up in the fuzzy high that the absurd proportions of her obsession didn't register until her neighbours began to complain of the noise.

The eviction notice that was slipped through the mail slot was still in her purse when she squatted in front of an enclosure in Room A, where a four-year-old bull terrier-fox terrier mix was sitting nervously on a sheet of pee-stained newspaper. The dog's eyes expressed a Buddha-like gentleness that wrapped Bailey in what felt like a warm dopamine suffused embrace, a connection that had her believing that the emotional wounds they had both endured had brought them together.

"He doesn't look like it, but he's a feisty bugger. You might want to watch your fingers."

Noah's presence always felt invasive—the way the animal rescue attendant tried so desperately to act younger than he was, the way he rolled up his sleeves to show off his biceps, the way he kept showing up when Bailey was alone. And yet, Bailey found herself excited by the power he so easily gave her.

"He reminds me of that logo from those old records," he added. "You know, the one with the dog and the gramophone?"

"A whatta-phone?" she said pulling her cellphone out.

"It's essentially the first record player," Noah said, casually placing an elbow on the top of the gate. "You're not too young to know what a record player is, right?"

She looked up for a split second, gave him an annoyed look, and then aimed her phone at the dog and took a picture through the bars. "Ooh, you are so cute," she cooed.

When she saw Noah staring, Bailey pulled her sleeve down to cover the exposed part of her arm.

"I love tattoos," he said. "I was actually thinking about getting one myself."

She took another quick photo and then looked up at Noah, whose eyes had moved to the skin where her collar narrowed into a V. Bailey knew that she was cloaked in the aura of her grief. She could tell by the way the world responded to her. It sometimes made people look at her with a deep concern, sometimes made them give her a wide berth, and sometimes seemed to make her invisible to everyone but dogs and horny men.

Turning back to the enclosure, she made a clicking sound with her tongue and opened the gate. "It's a sign of insecurity," she said as she attached the leash to the dog's collar, "when older men use references from their generation to feel superior over younger women."

As she walked away, her fingers were working on the keypad of her phone. "By the way," she said when she got to the door, "the image with the dog and the gramophone was called HMV—*His Master's Voice*. It was the official trademark of RCA Records." She dropped her phone in her purse. "You're not too old to know what Wikipedia is, right?"

The whistling kettle summoned Vanya to the stove where she turned off the burner and carried the kettle over to the table. As she poured the boiling water into the teapot, she began whispering a mantra honouring the goddess Annapurna. The prayer ended with her standing in front of the kitchen window gazing out at the neglected backyard. She felt a pang of sadness as she took in the earthy tumult of a once-vibrant garden. The lattice that had supported a dozen seasons of flowering peas, now cast a cross-hatched shadow over several varieties of tomatoes clinging desperately to their wilted vines. Further back, a cluster of peppers, a couple weeks past picking, had collapsed into a tangle of unharvested zucchini. The remains of the plot had been choked out by mouse-eared chickweed, spear thistle, ragwort, and yarrow. Beyond this, the wilting stalks of squirrel-ravished sunflowers lined the decrepit back fence.

Once a source of meditation and exercise for her husband, the garden now perfectly reflected his state of mind. Bouts of melancholy and episodes of disorientation had bloomed into a debilitating depression. When he refused the pharmaceuticals, Vanya took it upon herself to ensure that, like it or not, he took the meds the doctor had prescribed. As she poured Annu's evening tea into a small china cup, she stirred in the crushed selective serotonin reuptake inhibitors, added the honey and milk, and headed upstairs.

Even with the curtains open the room was dark enough that Vanya took each step slowly toward the bed, careful not to trip on a slipper, a book, or any other object her husband might have fitfully tossed onto the floor. When she got to the dresser, she put down the tea tray and turned on the bedside lamp. Annu was sitting up, three moves deep into a match of chess. The board resting across the striped leggings of his pyjamas tilted as he reached down and placed his trembling fingers on a rook. She watched him move the piece hesitantly, as if he was rethinking a strategy that took several hours to conceive.

"Chess in the dark," she said. "Annu, what is wrong with you?"

After nodding to his invisible opponent, he turned the board one hundred and eighty degrees and then settled back against the pillow. When he smiled at her, she couldn't help but smile back.

She took a certain pleasure in moments like these. Forty-odd years of marriage had taught her that despite their blustering and bravado, men were truly the weaker of the species. It could be witnessed in the simplest of moments. They're so vulnerable, she thought. Know-it-alls who, when it comes down to the things that really matter, know so very little.

Annu took a sip of tea, and steam rose up over his moustache to fog his glasses. Vanya watched him take them off, and as he rubbed the lenses with the hem of his pyjama top, she looked into the haze of his cataract eyes searching for the man she fell in love with all those years ago back in Kurnool. She could still recall the profoundly beautiful music that had drawn her through the crowded market that day, past carts full of mangoes, tamarind, and sweet lime, kiosks selling lottery tickets and tobacco, the tin stalls of meat, all the way to the rail station where Annu, dressed in a threadbare suit, was playing the violin next to a stone statue of a tiger. When their eyes met she was confronted by the undeniable certainty that she was standing before the love of her life. It was that simple. The music, his delicate hands, his posture, the sway of his torso, and the intensity of his gaze left her astonished and intoxicated all at once.

As Annu drifted into a half sleep, Vanya took the cup from his hands. The rest is history, she thought, her return to the train station the next day, Annu's acceptance in the Mehli Mehta's Bombay Symphony, eloping, and then the move to Canada when she became pregnant.

Vanya closed the bedroom door behind her, and as she carried the tea tray down the stairs, she felt the full burden of her family's welfare settle on her shoulders. For the sake of all concerned she turned her mind to the sraddha—Lord Ganesha, Ashwini Devatas, Mahavishnu, the seven holy rivers, and the matter of her grandson's soul.

Two

When Vanderlay found the single grey sock between the washer and dryer, he took a moment to look for its mate, and then tossed it into the garbage bin. He spent the next few minutes doing his best to neatly fold a fitted bedsheet, a particularly tedious and yet integral contribution to his *getting his shit together* goal. The moment he had the damn thing resembling the other folded sheets, he returned to the wastebasket. As he stared down at the discarded sock, it struck him as something profoundly sad, something representative of all the things that are diminished by the absence of its other. Discarded, abandoned, lost. It suddenly felt like his own life had become equally pointless.

The next thing he knew he was calling his wife, but the moment Aria answered, mentioning the sock seemed so ridiculous that he panicked and asked her about the laundry detergent. When he finally found the courage to tell her that he wanted her to come home, her agitation confirmed that he had to take the initiative.

A half hour later he was in the car with the paint sampler fanned out against the top of the steering wheel. He recalled that Aria had wanted something blue for the kitchen, but he couldn't remember the specific colour. Cobalt Glaze was too greyish. Midnight Navy, too dark. He was contemplating just how easy it was to get sucked into these home-improvement rabbit holes when his eyes fell on a swatch called Santorini Bliss. The Parthenon, a seaside villa, and the black-sand beaches of Perissa were to be the raison d'être of their Mediterranean-themed wedding twenty years ago: oregano-scented invitations, a spanakopita, calamari, and moussaka buffet. But he was half way through his residency at the time, exhausted, working seventy-hour weeks. He simply couldn't imagine anything more than a couple days at Niagara Falls and maybe another at a bed and breakfast sampling local wines. He remembered showing Aria a brochure with a heart-shaped tub. "It's the honeymoon capital of the world," he had said. She laughed. "I only plan on marrying once," she said. "I want to do this right." Not only did they never make it to Greece, but Vanderlay didn't accompany his wife on any of the trips abroad that she had taken. What he would give, he thought, to go back in time—their whole lives ahead of them, Aria in a white linen dress, the blue sea, a bottle of wine, a Mediterranean sunset. There was no one to blame but himself. Santorini fucking Bliss.

Vanderlay tossed the paint sampler onto the dash and eyed the ominous shade of grey that had now overtaken the sky.

In the Home Depot parking lot he pulled in between two oversized pick-up trucks. He couldn't help but notice their menacing grill plates, the dried mud splattered on the fenders: vehicles you had to climb into, designed as they were to proclaim a man's authority on the road. He gave a moment's thought to abandoning this mission in favour of heading to the grocery store for olives, but he forced himself to continue on.

The moment he passed through the automatic doors he felt woozy, out of his depth. As he took in the unsettling scale of it, he reminded himself that it was nothing more than a store selling the bits and parts that hold a house together, the bits and parts that we don't think about until they break down and have to be replaced. He aimed himself at a display of impulse items where he selected a pair of sunglasses with red plastic frames from a rotating carousel. As soon as he put them on, the dark lenses took the edge off.

He made his way toward the nearest aisle: air conditioners and humidifiers, furnace filters, vacuums. He kept moving: closet organizers, storage boxes, and bungee cords, a rack full of packing foam, duct tape, moving trolleys. A moment later he was wandering through a selection of laminate flooring. He turned down another aisle and passed a couple discussing a display of bathroom fixtures. The next aisle was blocked by a guy in a plaid shirt pushing a trolley loaded with two-by-fours. When was the last time I swung a hammer, he thought, or blew the sawdust off a freshly cut piece of wood? As he headed down the next aisle, he realized he couldn't even recall the last time he'd held a paintbrush in his hand. Tools began to blur in his peripherals: screwdrivers, wrenches, saw blades, tape measures, a long section of cabinet hardware, aluminum stepladders. Another turn: an employee filling a large barrel of blue plastic drywall anchors, shelves of nails, screws, hooks, hinges, fasteners, and then finally, an aisle of latex and oil-based primers.

He scanned the names of the paint cans towering above him. When he located the section of interior pastels, he was feeling vaguely vertiginous again. He reached back to steady himself, and his hand came in contact with a rack of spray paint. One of the cans fell to the floor, rolled in a slow circle and came to rest at his feet. As he bent down to pick it up, someone passed wearing the same grey wool socks as the one he had left in the trash. Once again the world was knocked out of plum. He straightened himself up and aimed himself at the exit.

He was several strides out the door when he realized that, not only was he holding the can of spray paint, but he was still wearing the sunglasses. He thought about turning around, but the anxiety he was feeling pushed him onwards. As soon as he got to the car, he slid into the driver's seat, reached over, and rifled through the glovebox, hoping he might find something that would calm him down. He found an empty bottle of tramadol, gave it a quick shake to be sure, and then tossed it back in the glovebox. He checked the console, checked the compartment in the door, and then gave the seat and floor a thorough look, just in case. He finally gave up and sat there staring out the windshield at the sky. The lead-coloured clouds were now smudged with a greenish hue. He took several deep gulps of air, and each breath nudged the horizon back into a steady plane. He started the car. "Just drive," he told himself.

He thought about heading for the highway—take that holiday everyone kept telling him he needed. Takeru had recently returned from Vegas and had recommended a round of golf at the Royal Links, the Barbra Streisand show at Caesars Palace, but none of these things interested him. His compulsion to just keep driving had less to do with a destination than it did with the desire to catch the skyline of the city in his rearview mirror, to satisfy an unspoken desire to leave everything behind.

After hitting three consecutive red lights, the siren of an approaching ambulance forced him to pull over. He sat there waiting for the vehicle to pass, its lights illuminated his car's interior, and something flashed in the rearview. He was about to turn and look when a honking horn steered his attention back to the road. He accelerated into the intersection and turned on the stereo. There was a Bud Powell disc in the player, but instead of piano, bass, and drums, he heard what sounded like thrashing guitars leaking from a pair of headphones. When he glanced in the rearview, there in the back seat he saw his son flickering like an image from an old film projector. He pulled into a plaza, parked, and leaned his head against the steering wheel until the heavy metal soundtrack was gone. Once he had calmed down, he took another deep breath and forced himself to look again. But this time there was nothing there but the plaza behind him, a run-down storefront with a flashing neon sign in the shape of a martini glass.

The *Closed* sign was flashing when Aria arrived at the music store. As she pulled at the locked door, Vincent, the store manager, looked up from the float he was counting, shook his head, and tapped the watch on his wrist.

"Please, please," she mouthed at him through the window.

He hesitated, but when she offered him an exaggerated look of desperation, he gave in.

Aria waited by a display of ukuleles as he locked the door behind her. Despite her suspicion that he probably still lived with his mother, she respected his expertise when it came to the subject of chordophones. "Thank you," she said, when he tucked the keys back in his pocket.

"Aria," he answered, "what can I do for you?"

"I need a violin."

"A violin?" he said, making his way back to the counter. "I just sold you one last week."

"It broke," she said.

"Not again."

"I know," she confirmed, "I'm terrible."

"Well, I'd love to help you, but you'll have to come back tomorrow," he said, sliding an arm into the sleeve of his blazer, "I have a show to get to, and there's a storm coming."

"I have to be somewhere too," she said. "I promise it'll only take a minute."

She watched him fuss with the collar and then start doing up the buttons.

"You have to help me." She said this like an unquestionable fact, but then added a softer, "It's an emergency."

She began to count to ten in her head. When she got to five, Vincent looked at his watch again, and then stepped out from behind the counter. "Okay," he said, "but we've got to be quick."

She harboured a mild loathing for men who could be so easily manipulated, but at that moment she had to resist the urge to give Vincent a hug.

She followed him to the back of the shop.

"We had a nice Karl Wilhelm on sale," he said dragging his fingertips along the curved shoulder of a Steinway grand. A few steps more and he was tapping the walnut casing of a Mason & Hamlin upright, "—but I sold it this morning."

She smiled, knowing that he was starting to ease into the cadence and rhythm of his sales routine. By the time they reached the woodwinds, he was acting as if he had all the time in the world. "Anyway," he said opening the door of the moisture-controlled showroom, "I take it you're still searching for the elusive seventh composition."

She couldn't remember mentioning this to him. Other than the fact that she had been in the shop several times in the last month, the details were pretty much a blur. "I am," she said.

They got to the burnished racks displaying the shop's violins, and he directed her toward a nicely flamed Heinrich Gill. "It has lovely tone," he said. "And it's also on sale."

As much as she appreciated his concern regarding the growing cost of these visits, she believed that the success of her quest could not be hindered by money.

She raised the instrument so that the ʄ-hole was next to her ear and then flicked the lower bout as if checking a cantaloupe for ripeness. She shook her head. "Too earnest."

Vincent hung the instrument back on the rack as Aria scrutinized a selection of Karl Höfners. She paused in front of a Guarneri 225.

"Good eye," he said. "Aged alpine spruce top, maple neck, not something you want to use as kindling though."

"I throw them against the wall," she said matter-of-factly, "I've never set fire to a violin in my life."

"Well, it's priced at five thousand nine-hundred and ninety-five dollars, but I can knock off twenty percent."

She knew he was trying to rush her now, but she was in the moment. When she leaned forward and inhaled, she got a hint of cherry followed by a tangy note of plated silver. A second later she was moving again, her eyes closed, her head tilted. Vincent followed until she stopped in mid-stride, turned, and smiled at the locked case.

"Mm, those are a little more expensive," Vincent said.

"That one there, second from the right." Her finger left a tiny smudge on the glass.

"That is a 1925 Boulangeot."

"It's beautiful."

Vincent looked at his watch again, "It's really getting late."

"Please," she said, "I just want to hold it."

He dug into his pocket for the key, and as he unlocked the cabinet door, Aria watched him hesitate for the second time since she had arrived.

"I really appreciate this," she said removing her jacket.

The moment she brought the violin to position, she inhaled a note of something ecclesiastical—wooden pews and dusty books—exactly what a violin should smell like. After a quick tuning, she abruptly riffed on a variation of the third movement of Tchaikovsky's violin concerto. Her style was vulnerable yet brash. She carved and quivered. One stroke was tender, the next was Napoleonic. Her hands moved, but in her mind she was sitting in a dark room listening to the instrument play itself, as if the violin was speaking to her, revealing its register, its timbre. So far, she had been inundated with countless stanzas of hesitating maybes. But then, somewhere in a long vibrato followed by a series of grace notes and staccatos, a resonating reply emerged, and for a split second she felt the sensation of being lifted into the air.

"I'll take it," she said.

Vincent laughed despite the fact that he didn't really think it was funny.

"I'm serious," she said.

"Do you have any idea what this violin is worth?"

She knew that somewhere inside he understood what she was looking for—she had seen him gazing lovingly at the pearl-white Bösendorfer Imperial concert grand. "Okay," she said, "how much for a down payment?"

"Aria—"

"Fine, then I'll rent it from you."

"I can't," he said.

In the brief moment that followed, she searched desperately for some kind of currency that might influence him. The thought of prostituting herself was quickly followed by the impulse to clobber him and make a run for it. "Let me borrow it until Monday," she said.

He was shaking his head again, but she could sense that he was distracted by something.

"Vincent, please. This is—" She hadn't intended to start crying, but when she did, she was aware of how his expression softened. A moment later it looked like he might start crying too.

"You have to swear that nothing will happen to this violin."

She wiped at her face with her sleeve and then placed her hand on her heart. "You have my word."

As she watched him select a Finn and Clay case with a humidifier and gyrometer—quality enough to protect the instrument without drawing too much attention to it—she felt the gravity of what he was doing. "I can't explain it," she said, "but you have no idea how much this means to me."

"I think I do."

Aria took the case with exaggerated care. "Until Monday."

At the door, Vincent hesitated for the third time and then took a step toward her. Aria was momentarily terrified by the idea that he might try to kiss her, or worse, change his mind about the violin.

"I'm late," she said, pulling the door open. "I really have to go." As she waved at him, she could see that he was trembling, the full force of his regret manifesting itself before her eyes. She turned to the street and flagged an approaching cab. "Thank you" she yelled. Reaching for the car door, she hoped that this violin, as special as it was, would survive the weekend.

❧

SPCA protocol clearly stated that walks of impounded animals were restricted to the building's fenced yard, but the coffee shop was right there, a block away, and Bailey was feeling the onset of a headache that only a latte would alleviate.

She had hoped the dog would appreciate the opportunity to go for a leisurely stroll outside of the small yard, but it spent the whole walk straining on the lead, as if it was hell-bent on getting somewhere. Bailey yanked back on the leash to heel the dog, and then, immediately regretting the reflex. She corralled him and began scratching him apologetically under the chin.

When she arrived at the coffee shop, she stopped to tie the leash to the trunk of a yellow-leafed sapling. She had just gotten down on one knee, when her phone began to vibrate. She tugged the buds from her ears, tucked her travel mug under her arm, and removed her phone from her purse. Her brother's name in the message window shoved her mind back to the night before—lying in bed, scrolling through her contacts, wondering who might be awake at 4 am. When she came to Dhani's number she couldn't help wondering what would happen if... She touched the screen, and before she knew it, the number was ringing—once, twice, three times. After the fourth ring the call went to voicemail. "Bisy Backson. Leave a message." There was no mistaking Dhani's recorded voice or the *House on Pooh Corner* reference. When the message prompt beeped, she panicked. "I miss you," she said, and then quickly hung up.

The incoming text, *I miss u 2*, made her breath catch. "What the hell?" she said aloud. She typed her brother's name followed by a question mark. Her eyes were fixed on the screen, when a sudden tug on the leash pulled her over. As she hit the sidewalk, her cellphone, travel mug, and purse tumbled across the cement. By the time she righted herself, the dog had already reached the end of the block and disappeared around the corner. "Holy fuck," she said. She turned to her things scattered on the ground. When she saw the crack running diagonally through the dark screen of her phone, she closed her eyes and waited for the full force of the wave to wash over her. Several seconds passed before she felt stable enough to move. She gathered her things and then stood there staring down the street in the direction the dog had disappeared. "Please come back," she whispered. A long spell passed before she realized she was holding her breath. As she exhaled she felt the full weight of the disaster settle on her shoulders. Not knowing what else to do, she turned and headed for the cafe.

She waited in line, taking a moment to assess the damage her phone had sustained. When it turned on, the crack in the screen was accentuated. She took a deep breath and touched the message button. The text from her brother was gone. She arrived at the counter feeling bewildered and deflated. "Latte. Double. For here," she said.

"May I interest you in a fresh pastry or muffin?"

Bailey knew that if she softened, even the tiniest bit, she would collapse into a sobbing mess. "Latte. Double. For here," she said again.

The server pointed at her travel cup. "Do you want me to put it in that?"

"I'm staying," she said turning her attention back to her phone. "I'd prefer a proper mug."

She had just confirmed that she could no longer text or call out when a coffee was placed in front of her. She watched the steamed milk being poured into the double shot of espresso, and a sudden rush of endorphins cleared her head. She said no to cinnamon, and yes to chocolate. As the coffee was being pushed toward her, she felt all the tension and anxiety give way to the anticipation of a caffeine-induced sense of well-being. But then, as the server pulled her hand away, the bangle on her wrist hooked the handle of the mug, and it toppled. Coffee spilled across the counter. Bailey stood there staring at this latest catastrophe, while the server grabbed a rag and started wiping up the mess, which plowed a portion of the milky puddle over the counter's edge onto the toes of Bailey's chestnut Uggs.

"Oops," the server said.

Her boots were well worn and out of style, but they had become precious and sentimental in a way she hadn't realized until she saw them stained with coffee. As the first tear of the day rolled down her cheek, she knew she was standing on the threshold of something pivotal—one of those fight-or-flight moments she had read about in a sociology class. In the end she just wiped at her cheeks and let another wave of disappointment crash against her.

Ten minutes later she was sitting on a stool in the front window with a replacement latte and a complimentary biscotti, staring at a wall of strange-coloured clouds on the horizon. Of course, she thought, rain—because this day wasn't already bad enough. There was only one place to take refuge. She typed in the cafe's wifi code and crossed her fingers. "Thank god," she whispered when the browser window opened.

She took a sip of coffee, a bite of biscotti, and soon enough the disappointment she was feeling was alleviated by the dozen red hearts on her latest Instagram post. An ongoing stream of selfies had given way to pictures she posted of the neglected animals that cycled through the shelter. Her most recent photo of a cross-eyed kitten had inspired several comments and two new followers, one from some Asian girl in Montreal and another from a photographer in Germany. She eventually moved on to her favourite gossip site. Between the articles about celebrity divorces and the photos of a makeup-less model caught shoplifting, she took several sips of coffee. As the latte began to do its work, an incoming message pinged on her broken phone. The relief that she could still receive texts was immediately crushed by the fact that it was from her boss, Jill. *Where are you?* it said.

Bailey checked the time. The SPCA closed in fifteen minutes. Her response, *Running an errand. Be back in 5,* resulted in an, undeliverable message, alert. She held down the *home* button. "Siri," she said, "why the fuck is this happening to me?" The reply, "Interesting question. I don't know the answer to that," was deeply disappointing. She grabbed her things, pushed in her chair, and then gave the empty mug a nudge. It made a satisfying sound as it shattered on the floor.

A scattering of sunflower seeds and tulsi leaves led from the kitchen table to the sink where Vanya was scrubbing a pot in warm soapy water. When she turned off the tap, she heard a muffled conversation coming through the ceiling. She recognized the musical prompts of Annu's favourite game show where the contestants phrase their answers as questions. Annu liked the host's snappy suits and the opportunity to test his knowledge in different worldly categories. She recorded the shows so that he could watch them on the small television in the bedroom when he felt like it, but for some reason, tonight, the distant voices felt like an intrusion, the tiresome banter of uninvited guests.

She turned on the radio to drown out the bothersome noise. A commercial for a fast-food franchise ended, and a woman began reporting the evening's breaking news: thunderstorms, record levels of precipitation, poor visibility, flooding, flight cancellations. Vanya was finishing the last of the dishes when the announcer mentioned the derailed train—*Two 400-pound Bengal tigers, part of the Ringling Bros. Circus, escaped when the cage they were transported in broke open in the north end of the city.* Her eyes went to the ceiling. Something creaked in the joist. She dropped the bowl she was rinsing into the sink and hurried up the stairs. She imagined the two tigers standing over Annu's body on the bed, the curtains and comforter torn to shreds, feathers from the bloodstained pillows fluttering in the air. She stopped at the top of the landing, tightened her grip on the bannister, and then headed back to the kitchen. She turned in a frantic circle until she located the broom. She ascended the stairs slowly this time, her breath rising as each step creaked under her weight. When she got to the doorway, she saw that the bed was empty. She poked the wooden end of the broom at the bed skirt, but nothing stirred.

"Annu," she called out.

A voice coming from the television responded. *What is a MacGuffin, Alex?*

She found her husband in the ensuite bathroom sitting on the toilet with his pyjamas around his ankles, his cupped hands covering his crotch. He looked up at her, his head tilting slightly to the left, then the right, as if angle and light might make the details a little clearer.

Vanya loosened her grip on the broom. "I'm sorry," she said and closed the door. A moment later she heard the toilet flush.

By the time Annu emerged from the washroom, she had swept a small cluster of dust into a pile by the door. She watched him shuffle over to the bed. He seemed confused and frail. She must get him to eat more, she thought.

When he eventually sat on the edge of the bed, he patted the spot beside him.

Vanya began to sweep again. "There's no time for sitting," she answered. The cadence of her voice matched the rhythm of her movements with the broom. "The sraddha is two days away."

Annu caught her arm as she passed. His grip was gentle but firm enough to stop her. She sat down with a heavy sigh. For a quiet moment the two of them looked out the window at the street together.

"What is troubling you?" Annu finally said.

"They're coming," she said. "One for you, one for Vanderlay."

Annu's eyes seemed to clear. "What are you saying?"

Vanya squeezed her husband's hand. "Tigers, Annu. The curse has found us."

Annu looked at her like a confused child. "There are no tigers in Canada."

"There are now," she said.

Three

The old man landed in the gravel at the side of the track in the CN yard just east of Union Station. As he scratched at his grey beard, he spotted a young guy in a pair of coveralls carrying a flashlight and a pair of wheel chocks—yellow handled wedges that he knew were used for securing railcars when they were being serviced. The rail worker tilted his hard hat and stared at the old man a moment before he came over and asked him what the hell he was doing.

"I'm trying to figure out how to get my gear down off this boxcar," he said."

He could see the guy contemplating whether he should radio this in. "Come on, son, there's a storm coming. Give me a hand, and I'll be on my way."

The rail worker looked back over his shoulder at the signal house and then dropped the chocks. He then hauled the backpack and a small trolley with a tool box and milk crate strapped to it out of the car and set it down.

"It seems to get heavier everyday," the old man said.

"I'll let it go this time, but don't let me catch you climbing on or off a train in this yard again. It's dangerous, and it's illegal."

"Don't worry, I won't be bothering you any time soon." The old man nodded toward the city. "The Hilton is that way, I suppose."

"The Hilton? Yeah, but they won't let you in dressed like—" The rail worker grabbed the wheel chocks and squinted at something in the distance. "Is that your dog?"

The old man turned to see a mutt standing on a pile of splintered skids staring back at them through the gloom. "I travel solo," he said.

As he heaved his gear onto his back, the rail worker crouched down and scooped up a handful of gravel. The old man didn't look back when he heard the dog yelp.

After hauling his belongings through the yard, he slid down a steep incline and then squeezed between a rusted fence pole and the footing of a concrete underpass. Once he was under the bridge, he dropped the pack onto the sidewalk and straightened his back with a groan. Cars thrummed by, the sound of their tires amplified by the concrete. He pulled out a well-used map, which he positioned under the orange glare of the light above him. Leaning in close, he located Anchorage, Alaska, and ran a finger along a purple line that cut across the southwest corner of the Yukon. He had followed the coast south through British Columbia before veering off through the Rockies to Alberta, where his journey carved diagonally across the flat grid of the Prairies to Winnipeg, and then zigzagged into northwestern Ontario to Thunder Bay. He uncapped a marker and made a fresh line along the top of Superior to Sault Ste. Marie, a long-haul rig lift skirting off the top of Georgian Bay into Parry Sound, and then a slow train to the outskirts of Toronto. After extending the line to his present location, he recapped the marker and traced a route with his finger down through Buffalo, New York State, and into Massachusetts. He was getting close. About eight hundred miles to go.

Vanderlay could feel the discomfort in his stomach the moment he entered the tavern. As he waited for his eyes to adjust to the dim lighting, he took in the low ceiling, the vinyl upholstered chairs, and the smell of stale smoke. There were three drinkers at the bar, one man and two women, watching the news on an old television. The bartender had her back turned, but Vanderlay could see her eyeing him in the mirror behind the shelves of liquor. To the right, an old mixing board, a microphone stand, two monitors, and four beer kegs occupied a small stage. On the other side of the room, a vintage jukebox blasting *Johnny B. Goode* splashed flashing light across the faces of two goth kids playing pool.

Vanderlay was just about to turn around and head back to the car, when the bartender strolled over and placed a small glass with a tea light inside it at one of the empty tables. "Just in time for Happy Hour," she said. "Everything on the menu is half price."

He took a seat, picked up the tea light and used it to illuminate a paper placemat decorated with classic 1970s cocktails—Harvey Wallbangers, Pink Ladies, Singapore Slings... He pointed at something called a Martini Americano. "Gin, if you don't mind. Dry, with two olives."

The bartender nodded and headed back to the bar.

The song on the jukebox ended, and the sound of a news report filled the room. Vanderlay turned to the television—a crowded street, police in riot gear, small fires. He was aware that he had no idea what was going on in the world anymore. Aria had taken the flatscreen, and he'd intentionally been avoiding the news on social media. He simply didn't have the bandwidth for anything more than the weather app on his phone.

When the bartender returned, Vanderlay nodded toward the television. "The world's going to hell," he said.

She placed a martini on the table. "In a handbasket, hon. That's why they invented Happy Hour." She took the ten dollar bill he offered her and then paused. "You okay?" she said, "You look a little pale."

Vanderlay forced a smile. "Nothing a martini can't fix."

She responded with a quick smile of her own and then strolled away without giving him change.

He wasn't expecting Bombay Sapphire, but when he took a sip it was obvious that what he got was vodka and that it wasn't even close to dry. He downed the martini and then pulled the single olive off the yellow plastic sword with his teeth. As he sat there waiting to see what affect the drink would have, he pressed his fingers into the four quadrants of his abdomen. While he was relieved to find there was no swelling or tenderness, this just confirmed that the pain was likely a physiological manifestation of unresolved emotional stress, a diagnosis that seemed more worrying than something that could be treated with a scalpel or antibiotics. After a discreet belch he got up and headed to the bar.

The three drinkers and the bartender were all staring at the TV. A woman in a tight-fitting outfit was gesturing dramatically at a map. *Unprecedented levels of precipitation are expected to continue over the next few days—*

"I'd like a Heineken," Vanderlay said.

The bartender shook her head at the screen and then pulled open the fridge door. "I knew I should have grabbed an umbrella when I left the house this morning," she said.

With a snap, the beer cap arced through the air and landed cleanly in a bucket. "Nine bucks," she said placing the bottle on the bar.

"Nine dollars?"

"If it isn't on the placemat," she said, "it doesn't qualify for Happy Hour, hon."

Vanderlay handed her a twenty. As he stood there waiting for his change, a quick report of gunfire drew his attention back to the TV. A journalist was standing in front of a heavily shelled wall, an armoured vehicle idling to her left. Her voice was calm, focussed, speaking to the camera as if the chaos around her was a backdrop on a stage. Something about the number of casualties in a village in Afghanistan scrolled across the lower portion of the screen. The image flickered. A soldier that looked just like Dhani appeared and then vanished again into a storm of static.

"Damn it," the bartender said. She reached up and started making adjustments to the antennae.

Vanderlay took a deep breath. The discomfort in his gut was moving now as if it had a determined purpose of its own. The bartender placed two five dollar bills in front of him. There was once again an uncertain expression on her face.

"You sure you're okay?" she asked.

I keep seeing the ghost of my dead son, he wanted to say, but he just forced another smile and took a long slug of beer.

He was about to head back to his table when the conversation between the three drinkers grew loud and animated. He heard the word, "predator," and then, "missing pets," rising above the din. The guy sitting between the two women took off his fedora and scratched the top of his bald head. "Coyotes, probably," he said.

The woman to his left looked worried. "Pets run away or get hit by cars all the time," she offered.

"Yeah, but we're talking about half a dozen missing cats and dogs in one day."

As Vanderlay guzzled back half his beer, a song that sounded like a mariachi band came on the jukebox.

"Excuse me," Vanderlay said.

The bartender, who was once again making adjustments to the antennae on the television, glanced at him. Vanderlay held up his bottle in one hand and indicated that he would like two more with the other.

She nodded and then gave the side of the TV a whack with the palm of her hand. The picture remained static-y but the sound cleared for a moment. *Authorities say the whereabouts of the two, six hundred pound tigers that escaped from Ringling Bros. Circus, is still unknown—*

"Can you believe this?" the bartender said. "Satellites and GPS tracking systems, and we can't locate a couple of tigers?"

"I'm not worried," one of the women at the bar said. She patted her hip as if she might have a concealed weapon tucked into her garter belt.

The bald guy leaned toward her. "Maybe we could use Vera as bait, catch the tigers and collect the reward. There must be a reward, right?"

He slammed his hand down on his knee. The nervous one on his left, presumably Vera, straightened up in her chair. "That's not funny," she said.

The guy put his fedora back on.

She shook her head. "I want an apology."

"I just meant that someone as delectable as you would surely attract the appetite of such an animal. Beauty and the beast, right?"

"Hey, hey, come on, no need to ruin the party," the other woman said. "Let's lighten things up, talk about something less serious"—she paused for effect—"like climate change or the bubonic plague."

As the bartender placed the two beers in front of Vanderlay, one of the goth kids pointed a cellphone at the bar and snapped a photo. "He still hasn't apologized," he yelled.

The bartender looked over at their dark silhouettes. "Out, both of you," she said, and then turned back to Vanderlay. "Eighteen bucks, hon."

As Vanderlay reached for his wallet, he watched the two kids pull a large black duffle bag out from under their table and then make their way toward the door. The lights from the jukebox illuminated something metallic protruding from the bag. Vanderlay couldn't guess what it was, but it reminded him of a contraption you might find in Frankenstein's laboratory—a thing that could be activated by a bolt of lightning. Very strange, he thought, as he pulled out another twenty.

When he got back to his table he placed the two bottles down in front of him, and collapsed into the seat. He was studying the cocktail menu when the song on the jukebox ended. Once again, the latest news report drew his attention back to the bar—*radar data as well as infra-red camera images confirm sightings of unidentified aerial phenomena over the city. While footage is compromised by meteorological conditions, reports say the object's movement and trajectory were erratic, unpredictable and otherwise anomalous—*

UFOs? Vanderlay thought. What's next? He decided that his next drink would be something called a *Corpse Reviver.* He had never had absinthe before, and it seemed like it might be just the thing to wake him from what was beginning to feel like an intensely surreal dream.

❧

"I'm so sorry for being late," Aria said.

"That's okay. It's just a couple of minutes."

Her therapist nodded at the violin case in Aria's lap. "I didn't know you played."

"I'm just getting back into it."

"I'm pleased. Music can be—I just realized—Aria—that's a musical term, isn't it?"

"It is. My father was a classically trained musician."

"Oh, that must have been a rich environment to grow up in."

Aria frowned.

The therapist frowned back at her. "We've talked about your marriage and your daughter, but this is the first time you've mentioned your parents."

"I don't think my parents are relevant."

"If you're not ready to talk about them, that's fine."

"I don't think it's a question of being ready or not. I just have more important things that I'm struggling with."

"I'm curious," her therapist continued, "you said that you're getting back into the violin, which suggests that you stopped playing for a period of time."

"It's been years."

"What happened?'

Aria sighed. "Are you sure you want to hear this?"

"We have fifty-two minutes," the therapist said, and she set the timer.

"The truth is, it was a rash decision that I made two decades ago found out that I was pregnant with Dhani." Aria could feel her blood pressure rising, a tension forming in her shoulders. "Looks like I'm going to be talking about my parents after all."

The therapist nodded encouragingly.

"When I went home to share the news, my mother doesn't even congratulate me, she just says, 'I guess I should have known this day would come.' Which obviously wasn't the response I was expecting. And then my father says, 'We always meant to tell you, but somehow it just never came up.'

"So I was sure they were about to tell me that I was adopted or something, but my mother starts talking about how our family is cursed. How whenever a woman in our family gets pregnant, the husband is killed. All the men, from my great-great-grandfather on down. And all by animals—a scorpion, a rampaging elephant, a cobra—apparently her father was killed by a buffalo.

"So, I'm looking at them in disbelief, and I ask my father, 'What about you? How did you manage to foil this supposed family curse?' But my mother interrupts, of course. She says, 'Leaving India and adhering to ritual and prayer are the only reasons he's alive,' and my father starts talking about how this is why it pains them so much that I've turned away from the gods that have protected them.'

"Then my mother reaches over and takes my hand, and she says, 'If you have this child, you must ask forgiveness of the gods you've abandoned, or you will put your father and your husband in great danger.'

"I couldn't believe they were associating the birth of my child with some superstition about the death of my father and my husband. Before I could stop myself, I was heading for the door, and I told them that I was quitting my position with the symphony. I know. It was childish and horrible, but it felt like the only real way I could strike back at them."

The therapist offered Aria a tissue box. "I'm sorry that you had to go through that, especially when you were an expectant mother."

"When I got home I talked to Vanderlay about it, but I just couldn't bring myself to mention the curse. It sounds ridiculous, but talking about it felt like it might make it real somehow. Vanderlay suggested that I wait until my maternity leave was over before making an important decision like leaving the symphony. But I told him that the baby had to be my number one priority, and he left it at that.

"I stayed up that night until four in the morning, researching everything I could find on prenatal care. I ordered three different books on maternal role attainment theory. By the end of the week I had lost myself in Lamaze classes, eco baby toys, audiovisual monitoring systems, bulk supplies of diapers, baby thermometers—you know, all the baby things. When my mother finally called to see how I was, I told her I never wanted to hear the curse mentioned again. She agreed, and I was so distracted by preparations that I almost forgot about it myself.

"But then, on the day Dhani was born, I couldn't get rid of the feeling that Vanderlay might really be in danger. It was there when I woke in the middle of the night and remembered that he was gone at the hospital. It was there every day as I was rushing around the house, trying to make the most of the time I had when the baby was napping. It was there in Vanderlay's voice when he recommended that we hire a nanny. It was there in my defensiveness when I said that I was quite capable of raising my own child. And it was there whenever I looked in the mirror. Look what's become of you, it said. You're a housewife.

"When Vanderlay sat me down and told me that I might be experiencing postpartum depression, I was a mess. We had a long, heated debate, but I eventually agreed to let my parents look after Dhani for a couple hours each morning.

During those mornings to myself I would just collapse in front of the television and binge travel shows that featured exotic luxury holiday destinations. Before long my anxieties about the curse and my regrets about quitting the symphony were buried under dreams of white-sand beaches, equatorial sun, and swimming with dolphins. But when I brought up the idea of a holiday, Vanderlay claimed he was too busy to take anything more than a couple days off work, which of course would limit our options to destinations within a few hours drive. We had our first real fight over that, but what could I say? I'd always known how important his job was to him.

"And then I went through the whole cycle of worry again when I was pregnant with Bailey. Doubling down on my travel obsession was the only thing that seemed to help. I cooked, I cleaned, I looked after my kids, and I dreamed of far away places. When Bailey was two, I brought up the idea of a holiday again. This time, Vanderlay saying no didn't upset me. I just told him that I was going with or without him.

"I spent a week on the Mayan Riviera and came home with a glow that everyone seemed to comment on. The moment feelings of regret and uncertainty began to cloud my head again, I went on another trip, this time to a wildlife reserve in Zimbabwe. A year later I was sleeping in a Sangrillo treehouse in the jungles of Costa Rica. While these trips invigorated me, the sense of well-being that I brought home from each destination always faded until the next one. And that's how it went for the next twenty years. Vanderlay worked, and I did everything I could to stuff the curse, along with all my family's cultural and religious beliefs, into a dark closet."

"I'm wondering," the therapist said, "are you close to your parents now?"

Aria looked down at the violin in her lap. "No," she said. "But it doesn't matter. I have more important things to deal with."

As Bailey headed off from the cafe, it felt like the world was crumbling around her. The dog, her phone, her apartment, and her job had gone from being things she had, to being things that were happening to her. And then it started to rain.

She ran until she reached the mall. She pushed through the crowd that had gathered in the concourse and made her way to the food court washrooms. She hung her purse on the back of a stall door, tore several feet of tissue from the roll, and carefully arranged it over the seat of the toilet. As she peed, she turned her attention to the graffiti markered on the walls: *Emily and Preston forever; Sexy kitten; Vote or Die.* She spent a moment trying to decipher a long illegible paragraph about a group called Pussy Riot, and then pulled her cigarettes out of her purse. Who needs the internet, she told herself. Toilet stalls are the original blogs. She lit the cigarette, took a deep drag and then blew out the match. The smell of sulphur and the blue wisp of smoke reminded her of a long-forgotten memory. She could almost feel the tingling sensation that had run down her neck when her brother pulled a shoebox out from under his bed and showed her his collection. She was old enough at the time to know that matches were dangerous, and yet all together like that, with their colourful covers, they seemed precious and beautiful. She watched him select a match book from the centre of the box and turn it in his fingers. "I got this one from the hotel lobby when we went to the Grand Canyon." *See it, to believe it*, the script said on the cover. He tore off a match and struck it against the black strip at the bottom of the pack. As it flared in his hand, his eyes went sort of calm and dreamy. He waited until it was just about to burn his fingers before he shook his hand and the match was extinguished. The smell of sulphur and the blue wisp of smoke.

"You can have it," he said, tossing the matchbook in her lap. "Once you use one, the pack has no value to a collector."

Surprised by this act of generosity she looked over at the closet. "Can I see the X-Men comics?" At the time they were the only thing he collected that she really had any interest in. She liked Storm and the blue shape-shifting woman.

Her brother stood up and turned to the shelves lining the wall of his room. "You can look at these," he said.

The pile of hockey cards that he handed her had a thick blue elastic band around them. She knew they were all doubles. He had the good ones hidden away in the closet, as well. She tossed the stack of cards onto the bed and was about to leave when he said, "I used to have a Sidney Crosby rookie card, but I traded it." When she paused, he added, "I bet you're wondering what I would trade a Crosby rookie card for."

Bailey shrugged her shoulders again, not understanding the gravity of what he was sharing with her.

"Close your eyes," he said.

She placed her hands over her eyes and watched him through the cracks in her fingers as he knelt at the heating vent, lifted the grill, and pulled out a balled-up grey sock. After it was unrolled, he reached inside and took something from it. “Okay,” he said, “you can look now.”

Not only was the bullet he showed her a lot bigger than she thought a bullet would be, but it had a strange, disturbing effect on her. “Where did you get it?” she asked.

“I told you, I traded someone for it.”

“For a hockey card,” she repeated, as if it would clear up the anxiety she was feeling.

“It’s a .303 calibre cartridge,” he said.

She imagined that it had some weight to it and that its pointy tip might even be sharp.

“You can hold it if you want.”

When he went to place the bullet in her hand, she pulled away, and though she wasn’t sure why, she began to cry. He turned to the shelves again. A moment later, he was standing in front of her holding a mason jar full of marbles. “You can have whichever one you want.”

She wiped at her face with her sleeve and watched him pour the jar out onto the bed. She selected a clear marble with a pink and yellow swirl inside. As soon as she put the marble in her pocket, she heard someone relaying a code on a radio, followed by a knock on the stall door.

“Excuse me. There’s no smoking in the washrooms.”

The idea of being escorted to the security office was one of the most humiliating things Bailey could imagine, but as they made their way through the food court, up the escalator and past her favourite shoe store, she was aware that no one even noticed her. By the time they had turned down a hall and entered the security office, she was more angry than embarrassed.

The office was a small white room with several computer monitors displaying the traffic in different parts of the mall.

“Code 43,” the guy who brought her in said.

A guard sitting in a chair watching something on his phone, raised a finger in the air. An eternity seemed to pass before he put his phone down and looked up. “Cat videos are so hilarious,” he said. He rolled himself over to the table full of monitors, grabbed a pad and pen, and then stared at Bailey for another uncomfortably long moment. "Smoking in a public washroom is a violation of by-law 32931," he said.

Bailey wondered if there wasn't a by-law that dealt with whether male security were allowed in women's washrooms, but she just wanted to get the whole ridiculous thing over with as fast as possible. "I'm really sorry," she said, "I promise I won't ever do it again."

"Not so fast," the security guard replied.

Bailey heard the door behind her close.

"Empty your purse."

"What?"

"Your purse. Empty it."

Bailey shook her head. "What is this?"

"It's protocol. And the sooner we get to the bottom of this, the sooner you can leave."

"The bottom of what?"

"Well, right now, your purse. Empty it, please."

Bailey looked around, but the only table in the room that wasn't occupied by surveillance monitors was several feet away and it was covered with the remnants of someone's half-eaten dinner. She extended her arms and dumped the contents of her purse onto the floor: a scattering of change, lip balm, a pack of matches, cigarettes, her wallet, her phone, tampons, the eviction notice, and an envelope.

"There," the security guy by the door said, pointing at the pack of cigarettes.

A few quick strides and he was standing over her things scrutinizing each item. When Bailey saw the tip of his shoe on the corner of the envelope it triggered a memory of the day the letter came into her possession. She had just secured the rope holding her mattress to the roof of her friend's car, when her father came out the door holding Felix, her threadbare stuffed dog. She was annoyed because she had intentionally left it in her room with the Barbie, the Harry Potter books, and the Winnie the Pooh videos. "Okay, let's go," she said. She hurried over to the passenger side door and climbed in, but her father tapped at the glass before her friend had put the car in gear. She had no choice but to roll down the window.

“There’s something I have for you,” he said.

She looked at the stuffed dog. “I’m not a kid anymore, dad.”

To her surprise, he took an envelope from his pocket. “I just found this in the mailbox,” he said. “It must have gotten lost or something.” He placed the stuffed dog in her lap and then offered her the letter. “It’s addressed to you.”

She stared at her name written on the front for second.

“It’s from Dhani.”

She suddenly felt strangely mortified, as if her father was offering her a piece of her dead brother’s blown apart body. Not knowing what to say, she stuffed the envelope into her purse. It had been there unopened ever since.

She got down on her knees and started shoving her things back in her purse. When she got to the envelope, the guard said, “What’s that, a love letter?’

Bailey got back to her feet. “None of your business.”

He looked a little taken aback by her tone of voice. “We could either let you go with a warning or we could ban you from the mall for six months—”

At that moment keeping it together was no longer an option, but there was no way she was gonna start crying either. “Fuck you guys.” The words surprised Bailey as they left her mouth. “Stop acting like you’re doing me some kind of a favour. You’re just a couple of power-tripping assholes.”

“Okay, have it your way,” the security guard said. “You are officially banned until—” he counted the months off on his fingers “—April. If we see you on the premises before then, you will be fined.”

Bailey slammed the door as hard as she could when she left, but instead of the thunderous exclamation she expected, the door just clicked softly behind her. She made her way through the mall feeling inconsequential, barely there, like she was slowly being erased from the world.

After taking a plate of food up to Annu, Vanya ate her own dinner that night sitting in front of the living room window, where she kept her eyes on the shadows around the neighbourhood hedges and fences. At some point a dark shape appeared at the top of the street. It wasn't clear who or what it was until a streetlight illuminated the filthy wet clothes of a guy carrying a couple of garbage bags. Vanya momentarily entertained the idea of inviting him in, letting him take a shower, sending him on his way clean and fed. But when he stopped at the foot of her lawn, lifted the lid of the recycling bin and started poking around, a sharp edge formed around her thoughts. She watched him as he rummaged about, making a racket and otherwise displaying a lack of regard for other people's property. The empty pickle jar and the plastic ginger ale bottle he was handling were not that long ago in her fridge, she thought. The invasiveness of it, the feeling of trespass awoke in her a need to establish the lines of her defence. There were tigers loose in the city. Tigers that she was certain were at that very moment making their way to her house. Before she had time to consider what exactly it was she planned to do, she was on her feet and heading for the front door with the broom in her hand.

By the time the guy saw her coming it was too late. The broom struck him flush across the side of his jaw. He stumbled and then collapsed onto the wet road. Vanya was standing over him with the broom raised in the air. "I'm so sorry," she said, "I thought you were—" her voice trailed off, "something else."

She watched him get up slowly and back away, the bottles and cans in the bags he was carrying clinking as he retreated. She turned back to the house—just a pane of glass, she thought, between safety and the wild and dangerous things lurking out here in the dark. She hurried inside, made her way to kitchen, and called her son-in-law.

Four

The alley the old man had set up in was optimal considering the conditions that working on the road usually allowed. It was close to the stadium where a big game was letting out, there was an electrical outlet next to the dumpster, and despite the light rain, the foot traffic going by was heavy.

"Evening, boys," he said to the two guys looking at him from the sidewalk.

"Is that a tattoo gun?" one of them asked.

The old man turned on the headlamp he was wearing and looked down so that the beam of light was shining on the thing in his hand. "Tattoo machine," he said.

"You tattoo out here?"

"Right here and now if you're interested," the old man said, illuminating the power supply, the bottle of antibacterial soap, the alcohol.

"Does it hurt?"

"Mmm-hmm."

"How much?"

"How much does it hurt, or how much does it cost?"

"Both, I guess."

"As far as the pain goes," the old man said, "as long as you stay away from the ribs, I'm sure you'll be fine. The price depends on what you want."

The guy asking the questions was now under the tarp with the old man, looking down at the gear, most of which was covered in sterile bags.

"What's with all the plastic?" he asked.

"I take cross-contamination very seriously."

"How long does it take?"

"That, too, depends on what you want."

"I'm outta here," his friend called out from the sidewalk.

For a second, the old man thought he'd lost his customer, but the guy didn't even look when his friend walked away.

"I was thinking of getting my daughter's name on my arm."

The old man sat him down on a tool box and then took a seat himself on the milk crate.

"What part of the arm do you want it on it?"

The guy pointed at the middle of his bicep.

The old man pulled the cap off a marker and got to work on the stencil. "What's your daughter's name?" he asked. He had done enough banners with roses in his lifetime that he could practically work with his eyes closed, and yet, he still treated every tattoo like it was the last one he would ever do.

"It's not gonna be purple, is it?" the guy asked, scrutinizing the design being drawn on his arm.

The old man nodded at the box of inks. "The outline will be black, the roses red, and the leaves green."

When the stencil was done, the guy flexed. "Looks good."

"Check the spelling," the old man said.

When he got the nod, he put the marker away. "A hundred and fifty bucks."

After checking all his pockets, he stood there a moment counting the money in his hand. "I only have a hundred and thirty-eight...fifty."

The old man took the money, tucked it into his sock, snapped on a pair of nitrile gloves, and went to work. The routine eased the ache in his bones, slowed his heart rate, aligned its erratic beat with the pulse of the machine.

When he paused to wipe away the ink and blood, the guy asked him how long he had been tattooing.

While many of the details of his life were beginning to blur, he could still clearly recall the day when it all started. He was eighteen with a mad crush on Bettie Page and eighty-five dollars in his pocket when he ran away from his drunk father, stole a car, and drove to New York. He found himself on the Coney Island boardwalk back when Steeplechase and Shoot the Freak were still around. The beaches were jammed with weekend vacationers and local gangs. The whole place made his head spin. He woke up the next day with a brutal headache and a giant eagle on his chest. As he stared at the tattoo in the mirror, the initial shock gave way to a sense of pride. The tattoo spoke of something that he'd been feeling his whole life but had never been able to express. It was a fuck you, but it was more than that. He felt like he had grown a foot taller. He headed back to the boardwalk that afternoon with the name Smokey Jackson clanging about in his pounding skull. When he found Smokey's shack, he placed a bottle of whisky in the tattooer's hand and grabbed a broom. He swept the floors, lit Smokey's cigarettes, and otherwise kept his mouth shut. At the end of the day he stood the broom up in the corner and said goodnight. He showed up the next day, and the one after that. Smokey never said a word to him, neither kind nor foul, until the day a big fella came into the shop claiming that Smokey had tattooed the wrong name on his girl's breast. When he saw the knife, he picked up an empty whisky bottle and broke it over the sailor's shaved head. "All right," Smokey said, as if he had just noticed him for the first time, "I can see you already know what to do with a broom and whisky bottle, but can you handle the real customers, and I'm not talkin' about the bums that you gotta throw out, I'm talking about the paying ones." Smokey paused and ran a freshly licked thumb across his eyebrows. "It's not rocket science. All you need to do is ballpark the prices, allow for variables. There are almost always variables—cash only, always up front—no exceptions. And you'll need to be able to take a machine apart and put it back together blindfolded before you even dream of tattooing anyone."

He spent his evenings hustling eight-ball and snooker so that he could afford to get more tattoos. In those days it was all banners and hearts, panthers and eagles, three-mast schooners and hula girls, along with the odd dragon and geisha. He watched Smokey work and began to slip in the odd question, but Smokey wouldn't give him a straight answer. "Loose lips sink ships," he kept saying. "Just pay attention."

He tattooed his first customer a year later. He was tightening a freshly cut spring onto the armature bar of a machine he had built from a crate of parts he found in the back of the shop when a guy came in wanting a mermaid tattoo. Smokey was passed out in the bathroom, so he took a belt of whisky and got to work. When he was done he put the money in the jar and placed it in the drawer under the counter. This went on for weeks, until one of the guys he'd tattooed came back into the shop for more. Smokey scrutinized the work he'd done, and then, when the customer left, he shoved him up against the wall. "Now I want you to pay attention," he said, "I get sixty percent of everything you make. Don't even think of holding out, or I'll break your fingers and toss you back in the gutter where I found you."

He became known as the evening shift at Smokey's shop. It was like a dream to be making money, having so much fun, and it was all legal to boot. There were lots of fights, and he lived the life, working hard and then drinking hard. His head was full of pirates and booze and women, and he was in love with the freedom and satisfaction of seeing his customers so proud and ready to take on the world simply because he had hammered a solid and decent image into their bicep.

And then someone left that damn book in the shop. He found it there on the back of the toilet one day. When he asked if Smokey knew anything about it, Smokey glanced at the cover. "Never seen it before."

At first, he found the book difficult to read, long wordy passages about trees and hilltops, but on page ninety-seven it got interesting—*I was not born to be forced. I will breathe after my own fashion... when I meet a government which says to me, 'Your money or your life,' why should I be in haste to give it my money? It may be in a great strait, and not know what to do: I cannot help that. It must help itself; do as I do. It is not worth the while to snivel about it. I am not responsible for the successful working of the machinery of society.*

And that was the end of it. Those words spoke of an alienation toward a system that claimed ownership of everything. He had set out on the road because his old man was a prick, and because working and paying bills felt like a prison, and now in a way, Smokey owned him. The booze and the money owned him. It was all just another trap, all of it. The next day he told Smokey he was done.

The long and short of it was, he never worked for another man. He started tattooing on the road, bartering his work for food, lodgings, or whatever else he needed. By the time he was thirty he'd seen most of Europe and had even been to Japan to visit the grave of the master tattooer, Horiuno.

After all these years his machines felt like old and trusted friends who had travelled the world with him, and in moments of creative concentration he would even go as far to say that they felt like an extension of his mind, and yes, his own body. He was in fact reminded every time his heart palpitated that the machine was, simply and profoundly, like himself, just another thing with an undetermined shelf life.

The old man had just finished shading the leaves of the roses, when the garbage bin under the fire escape was cast in a muted red, blue, and white strobe. The old man put the machine down gently and raised his hands in the air as if he had been caught red-handed cracking a safe. His customer jumped up, scanned the alley for a quick escape, and then sat back down on the tool box.

"Good evening boys," the old man said with a sigh.

"What do we have here?" one of the cops said.

The beam of the flashlight fell on the tray of ink, the sharps container, and the bag full of ink-stained paper towels, and then paused on the tattoo.

"Looks like some illegal back-alley activity."

"Just doing a little business," the old man said, peeling off the nitrile gloves.

"I'd say you're breaking at least ten codes of public health."

"Everything's sterile and bagged, and the needles and tubes are one-use disposable."

"We're going to need to see some ID," the cop said.

"Let me get this bandaged up."

When he was done he went over the aftercare instructions, and then sat back down. "I lost my ID this morning," he said.

The customer was released on the recommendation that he go to the nearest hospital and get blood work done to make sure he hadn't been infected with HIV or hepatitis or god knows what other micro-bacterial horrors might be lurking in the alley.

They allowed the old man to pack all his gear up before they cuffed him. He went quietly. He always did.

❧

When the bartender cut Vanderlay off, he staggered over to the washroom. The wave of embarrassment he was fleeing was there waiting for him when he stopped at the sink and stared into the mirror. His reflection looked vaguely alien. Instead of the confident and approachable person he envisioned, he saw a man who looked a little ragged and uncertain, a man who had just told three strangers about how his sleep was plagued by flying dreams that left him feeling as if gravity was nothing more than a tyranny of the mind, a concept that could be overcome by a combination of sheer will and complimentary wind conditions. How bone mass, weight ratios, and flight feathers aside, he would sometimes wake up feeling like Icarus, both exhilarated and frustrated because his ability to fly was often accompanied by some kind of limitation. Sometimes he could only stay aloft for a few yards at a time. Sometimes he had the sense that something heavy was weighing him down, and then, of course, there was the damn sun. And yet, once in a while, he was able to fly uninhibited by these anxieties and soar with exhilarating control and speed over acres and acres of corn, wheat, and soy that gave way to a dense forested area surrounding a small blue lake. These dreams were sometimes so lucid it could take several minutes before the full weight of his burdens once again filled the hollow of his skeleton.

Vanderlay knew this was all just a symptom of the things he couldn't bring himself to face, and that offering it to strangers as an unsolicited biography was making his grief public. It was a proof that his ability to manage things was in question.

He splashed some cold water on his face, pushed the door open, and as he staggered toward the exit, felt the weight of his embarrassment and shame.

❧

The cab was driven by a man with a Middle Eastern accent. "Good evening," he said, "and welcome aboard."

Aria rolled up her sleeve and read out the address of Oliver Silverman, a man who claimed to have been abducted by aliens while playing a round of golf during his annual Florida vacation. The blog on his website emphasized the *suddenness* of his experience—how the ball he had hit *suddenly* vanished over the fairway, how the temperature *suddenly* dropped, and then how he felt himself being lifted *suddenly* into the air. She was certain that Oliver Silverman was just another crackpot, but when she came to the part that mentioned how he had heard music, which he described as, "classic, epic, and deeply heartfelt," she impulsively sent him an email and arranged a meeting.

"Bad weather is coming," the driver said.

"Yes," said, turning to the window, "it doesn't look good."

"If you don't mind me saying, ma'am," he added, "it is a pleasure to have a passenger as lovely as yourself in my cab."

Aria was used to the flirtations of strangers, especially from men who couldn't seem to contain their own desperate loneliness, but it bothered her when these men threw their opinions around so freely. This was a business transaction not a dinner party.

"Let me guess," he said, "you're from India?"

"My parents," Aria said.

"I would say Andhra Pradesh. Am I correct?"

Aria was in no mood for such banter, even if he had somehow named the state her parents were from.

"Beautiful country, India. I was there once when I was a boy."

"I've never been," she said. "I was born here."

"Born here, but the blood in your veins comes from your ancestors. There is no escaping one's cultural history."

Aria frowned. All she wanted to do was get to her destination and get what was beginning to feel like a ridiculous waste of time over and done with.

The driver was looking in the rearview again. "I am from Iraq. It is in my country where the first writing system was born, mathematics, astronomy, written law. This is all part of who I am."

Aria found herself wondering if he was a refugee, if he too had lost someone close to him—a wife, a parent, a son. She turned back to the window just as the first few drops of rain began to fall.

"It can be very hazardous," the driver said, turning on the wipers, "this taxi driving. Inclement weather, traffic accidents, angry passengers—"

In the absence of her response a quiet moment passed, but before long, she could feel the driver's eyes again.

"I would like to offer you my business card," he said. "Next time you need a cab you can ask for me by name."

As soon as she took the card, the heavy rain and the muffled sound of her phone now ringing in the pocket of her jacket, struck her as a chorus of invasive forces. "Listen," she replied, "I don't mean to be rude—" She glanced at the name printed on the card, "—Mister Ja-far-i, but I'd appreciate it if you'd just—"

She dropped the business card onto the floor, leaned her head against the rain-streaked window, and retreated into the sedating lull of the passing cars, honking horns, and wet hissing thrum of the city.

When the cab finally pulled up to the curb, the driver leaned over the seat. "We have arrived safe and sound," he said.

She could tell by the look in his eyes that she had hurt his feelings. "How much do I owe you?"

"The fare is twenty-six dollars, please."

Aria handed him two twenties. "I'm really sorry for being so rude."

"I understand," he said, "sometimes silence is better."

As he began to count out her change, she told him to keep it, and climbed out of the cab.

She checked the address again, then hurried over to a door next to a flower shop and rang the bell. When the door opened, she was greeted by an older woman in a housecoat. "So nice of you to come in such terrible weather," she said.

As the woman led Aria up to the apartment, she related that her husband had been suffering from severe migraines ever since the abduction and that his only relief seemed to be grape popsicles. At the landing she opened another door and led Aria into what was a cluttered hallway filled with boxes, stacks of magazines, unopened mail, four winter tires, and an uncountable number of egg cartons. At the end of the hall she knocked at what appeared to be a bedroom door.

"Are you sure it's okay to disturb him?" Aria asked.

"Oliver was actually out of bed for an hour or so this evening. He felt well enough to join me in the kitchen for dinner." She pushed the door open. "It's been a very good day."

The only light was coming from the hall behind them, but Aria could see that the room was filled with fans, each pointing in a different direction. As her eyes continued to adjust, the shape of a large man sitting up in a king-size bed came into focus.

"Honey," Mrs. Silverman said, "this is that lovely woman we were talking about."

"Oh yes, yes, come in." Oliver's baritone voice seemed to shift and blow around the dark room.

Aria tiptoed through the mess of extension cords and stopped at the foot of the mattress. The crosswinds from the fans made it difficult to find a position where her hair wasn't blown into her face.

Oliver cleared his throat and apologized. "The fans keep the room cool, but more importantly, they, pardon my language, fuck up the alien tracking systems." He looked up and pointed at the ceiling. "They track their abductees, you know. Once they do their work on you, they keep a close watch." He began to vigorously rub his temples. "The other thing that works is water. There are absolutely no documented cases of a person being abducted while swimming."

"I don't want to take up too much of your time," Aria said as she took out her phone, "so I'd like to get down to business."

"Are you sure you weren't followed?" he asked.

Aria hesitated. "I don't—no," she said.

"No, you weren't followed, or no, you aren't sure?"

She stepped further into the dark room. "I just need you to listen to something." She had to move two of the fans in order to get close enough to hand him the ear buds. "I need to know if this is the music you heard when you were—"

As he reached forward, he groaned like a creaking piece of timber in an old ship. "I never put this part on the website," he said, settling back. "But the experience left me with—" He inserted the buds into his ears. "Let's call it, extrasensory powers."

She was searching the menu for the playlist with the six compositions when Oliver raised his hands in the air and began making gestures as if he was conducting a symphony. "This is definitely the music I heard," he said loudly.

Aria looked back at her phone. She hadn't even hit the *play* button yet.

"I remember now," he said. "This is definitely the music that was playing during my abduction." He pulled out the earbuds, bunched them up in his fist. "The song is called "Bohemian Rhapsody", but we mustn't indulge ourselves as these devices can be traced."

Aria stuffed her phone back in her purse, hurried through the maze of fans, and quietly closed the door behind her. As she made her way down the stairs she pushed up her sleeve, licked her finger, and vigorously rubbed at the address written on her arm. "Another damn dead end," she whispered.

Once outside she pulled up the collar of her jacket, and, as she peered out at the dark wet streets, she realized that she was praying—words she thought she had forgotten in a language she hadn't spoken in years.

Bailey shoved the mall door open and stepped out into the drizzle. When she spotted a westbound streetcar about a block away, she turned toward the nearest stop. She came upon a homeless person with a dog curled up on a wet piece of cardboard and reached into her purse for some change. The dog looked up at her with the saddest eyes she had ever seen, and she knew she couldn't go home. A moment later she was posting the picture of the dog on her IG—#missingdog #rainsucks, #K9love. By the time the streetcar passed, three hearts had already appeared on her post.

Her aimless search eventually took her to a city park, where the sound of a barking dog drew her attention to a stand of trees. She headed across the wet grass to investigate, and there among a group of cedars was one of those poodle mixes, squatting next to an older gentleman smoking a pipe. The disappointment she felt was interrupted by the banter of three guys wearing baseball caps converging on two goth kids pushing a shopping cart along the lit path at the bottom end of the park. The pair were unaware that they were being stalked until an empty pop can struck one of them in the back of the head. As the kid awkwardly patted at his black-dyed hair, the three jocks ran up and blocked his path. Before she knew it, Bailey was marching toward them.

"What's in the bag?" the guy who threw the can asked.

"Leave them alone," Bailey said.

Taking advantage of the distraction, the two goth kids turned and ran.

Bailey positioned herself behind the cart.

"What if I don't?" the guy asked.

His two friends started to laugh.

Bailey bit her lip and shoved the cart forward as hard as she could. It slammed into the guy's knees, making him step back awkwardly and then collapse onto the ground. As he sat there swearing, one of the other guys walked up on her. She aimed her boot at his crotch, but he swung at her before her foot made contact. The next thing she knew she was on the ground, and the guy who hit her was standing over her, calling her things that derogatorily referred to both her gender and the pigment of her skin. As she stared up at him, something that sounded like Peruvian panpipes drew her attention to the black duffle bag in the cart.

The guy who hit her, turned. "What the hell is that?" he asked.

"His Master's Voice," Bailey whispered.

When the guy on the ground called out, his two friends went over to help him up. Bailey knew that she should take that opportunity to get out of there, but instead she just got to her feet, lit a cigarette, and watched them carry the guy over to the cart. They removed the bag, placed it gently on the wet path, and then loaded their injured friend in its place. When this was done, the bag was placed on his lap, and the three of them headed off.

Bailey stood there in the drizzle feeling the adrenaline dissipate, and with it went what remained of her hope. She flicked her cigarette into a puddle and turned in the direction of home.

A block and a half later she spotted the three guys at the entrance of a nearby hospital. One of them was helping the inured guy get to the emergency doors, while the other one grabbed the cart and headed back toward the sidewalk. Bailey retreated to a phone booth across the road where she watched him park the cart in the bushes. Once it was hidden, he went over to the Emergency Entrance sign and took out his phone. When it became clear that the kid was guarding the cart until his friends returned, Bailey pushed the phone booth door open. Just then, a mangy raccoon trotting across the street was silhouetted by the headlights of an approaching car, the car skidding to a stop just inches shy of running it over. She watched it make its way to the curb, feeling a renewed sense of urgency, as if a clock was ticking, marking the passing of each precious second of what remained of her own life. She turned back to the phone booth.

Calling Noah meant that she was probably involving herself in yet another regrettable situation, but he knew how to find missing animals. If I can do this one thing, she told herself as she jammed a dollar into the slot, I will never tell another lie. I will give up smoking, go back to school, anything.

The phone rang several times before Noah finally answered. It sounded like she had woken him, but he brightened when he realized it who it was. Before she knew it, the drama of the day came flooding out: the fight in the park, getting banned from the mall, her impending eviction, and, finally, the dog running away.

"Okay, just calm down," he said. "I can meet you in a half hour."

She had just given him her address when the guy minding the shopping cart took off toward the Emergency doors. A moment later the phone booth was flooded with the lights of an approaching cop car. Bailey's impulse was to run as well.

Having been assaulted earlier that evening by a crazy lady with a broom, the guy with the bags of scavenged bottles and cans was nursing a vertical root fracture, which was making his already compromised life practically unbearable. The pain radiating through his jaw and up into his temples had gotten so bad that he was considering the advice of a fellow down-and-out soul, who assured him that he knew exactly what needed to be done.

The logic in his friend's proposed method of dealing with the aching tooth hinged on the absolute certainty that emergency dental clinics, if they were in fact open at this time of night, would never perform the removal without the hundreds of dollars the procedure would cost. "I, on the other hand," he said, reaching into the knapsack he was carrying and pulled out a vinyl shaving bag, "can solve your problem, pro bono, here and now."

The one with the aching tooth was holding a *Renter's News* magazine over his head. "Okay," he said. "Just don't make me regret this."

His friend proceeded to empty the contents of the shaving bag onto the top of a blue box. "Don't worry about a thing," he said, slowly extracting an arm's length of dental floss.

"Woah, what are you doing?"

"It's no big deal, I've done this a hundred times."

His friend was surprisingly efficient as he lassoed the ailing tooth, tied a knot, and then secured the other end of the floss to the blue box handle. He was then given a solid punch in the arm. "Trust me, you're gonna thank me when this is over."

"I don't know about this."

"On the count of three. One. Two—"

The door was yanked open so forcefully that for a moment it looked as if he was peering over the edge of a cliff. When he finally steadied himself, a long clot of saliva and blood spilled out of his mouth.

"Fuck," he said, reaching for the broken strand of floss hanging over his chin. "It's still in there. And now I'm bleeding to death."

"Holy shit," his friend said, slowly backing away.

The guy with the floss hanging over his chin swiped at the contents of the shaving kit, sending the tweezers, nail clippers, scissors, and tooth brush, skittering onto the wet sidewalk. He then picked up the plastic bags filled with bottles and beer cans, and started walking away.

"Where are you going?" his friend yelled.

The blood pooling in his mouth made it hard to answer. "To the hospital," he said. "Where I should have gone in the first place."

By the time he arrived at the top of the drive leading to the Emergency entrance, he was already having second thoughts. He looked down at the bags in his hands, the blood on the front of his shirt, and turned back to the road. When he got to the curb he heard the muted melody of an old blues song. He stood there in the rain with an incessant throb in his jaw, and it dawned on him that the mournful strains of Blind Willie Johnson's guitar had been playing somewhere in his head his whole life.

He spat out another mouthful of blood, then gave the floss a sudden and desperate yank. He had a crazed and bloody smile on his face when the headlights of a passing car illuminated the shopping cart tucked away in the bushes next to him.

Five

From the back window of a patrol van, the cubically layered design of the police headquarters reminded Vanderlay of a hillside favela his wife once photographed while visiting the less-fortunate parts of Brazil. The vehicle circled down the drive of the precinct and stopped in front of a steel door, where the driver tapped the horn three times. The van proceeded into the garage, and Vanderlay felt as if he was being swallowed for the second time that day.

Once inside the precinct, Vanderlay and the group of men he was sharing the van with marched single file through what looked like the shipping wing of a convention centre. The cop leading the way took them to the processing room, where another door slammed closed. A voice ordered them to step back behind a yellow line. After a moment of chaotic shuffling, Vanderlay found himself leaning against a white brick wall. He did his best to stand up straight and focus on the four officers who, shoulder to shoulder, formed a solid barrier of authority. One of the cops took their names and addresses, asked if they had any allergies or medical conditions, and then ordered them to remove their shoelaces, belts, and, in Vanderlay's case, his tie and sunglasses as well. These articles, along with wallets, keys, and cellphones, were placed in clear plastic bags, which were labelled and tossed on a table. Vanderlay was finding it increasingly difficult to keep his balance, until one of the officers put on a pair of latex gloves, and as the inspection moved from his hair, to his mouth and ears, down to the soles of his shoes, the fog in his head gave way to a sobering wave of humiliation.

Once these proceedings were complete, Vanderlay and an old guy with a long grey beard were separated from the others and led down a hall into a cell.

Another door slammed closed.

“I want my phone call,” Vanderlay yelled.

The words sounded pathetic echoing down the corridor.

“You might as well make yourself comfortable,” the man said.

When Vanderlay turned around, his cellmate was laying down on the bench, using his cardigan as a makeshift pillow.

“You won’t be going anywhere until morning,” he added.

The idea of being stuck in jail all night settled heavily on Vanderlay’s mind. Okay, he told himself, if this is happening, I need to make the best of it. He took a couple uncertain steps across the cell, offered his hand, and introduced himself.

The old man looked up at Vanderlay with a suspicious look on his face.

“I’m sorry to intrude,” Vanderlay said, “but if we’re stuck here for the next four or five hours, we might as well know each other’s names.”

“HD,” the man said, giving Vanderlay’s hand a quick shake.

When HD laid his head back onto the bench and closed his eyes, Vanderlay returned to the other side of the cell. He massaged the red marks the cuffs had left on his wrists, then took a moment to assess his surroundings. The lower half of the two-tone walls were painted a dingy grey, which gave way in a precise horizontal line to something he recognized as Builder’s Beige, an uninspiring pairing of colours intentionally designed, he thought, to signify that you were now in a place of practicality and seriousness. The cement floor, which showed visible traces of hardened vomit, dry urine, and a number of other fluids, confirmed the diagnosis. He looked up at the ceiling and spent a long moment trying to imagine a clear, star-filled sky.

He wasn’t conscious of the fact that he was testing the solidness of the floor with his heel until the old man cleared his throat. “I once shared a cell,” he said, maneuvering himself onto his side, “with a fella who knew every lyric Lennon and McCartney ever wrote. Annoyed the hell out of me.” He took a moment to reposition the cardigan under his head. “Some folks while away the time singing, some tap dance, me, I prefer sleeping.”

Vanderlay knew that getting some sleep was probably a good idea, but there was nowhere else to sit, let alone lie down. "I was just wondering..." he began.

The old man's exaggerated sigh reminded Vanderlay of his daughter's habit of expressing annoyance every time he intruded on her life.

"Why do you suppose they took our shoelaces?"

HD made another adjustment to the cardigan before he replied. "You'd be surprised what a desperate man can do with a bit of string."

"Not that I'm suggesting anything," Vanderlay said, "but if a person wanted to harm themselves, they could quite easily use the sleeves of your sweater."

"Well," HD replied, "if you start feeling suicidal let me know."

Vanderlay was moving again, counting each step across the length of the cell. When he reached the back wall, he stopped and pressed his forehead against the cement. The cool flat surface was strangely comforting.

"You know, being in jail isn't the end of the world."

Vanderlay turned from the wall. HD had a look of concern on his face.

"Maybe you're right," he answered. "When you consider how many people at this very moment are being diagnosed with malignant tumours or," his voice got quiet, "being blown to pieces by crudely made bombs, or whatever else, I guess being in jail is a relatively minor inconvenience."

HD sat up. "Sounds like you need this bench more than I do."

Vanderlay shuffled across the cell. The moment he sat down, the lights seemed to brighten. He took HD in with a more focussed eye, could see that his clothes, though worn, were surprisingly clean. There was also an odour reminiscent of a summer shed—grass clippings and gasoline. "I know it's none of my business," he said, "but what kind of trouble brought you here?"

"They got me for vagrancy," HD offered, "a bunch of health code infractions, and something about, 'unlawful use of pirated electricity'." He leaned his head back against the wall and then dragged his fingers through the length of his beard. "Anyway," he added, "it's no real bother, with the rain and all, saves me the hassle of finding a shelter for the night."

Details surrounding Vanderlay's own arrest were coming back now—stumbling out of the tavern into the rain, climbing into his car, realizing he was in no condition to drive. And then, just as he was about to recline the seat and sleep it off, he saw an army recruitment ad at the far end of the parking lot. Even as a memory, the aftershock was wreaking havoc on his heart. "I vandalized a billboard," he said. "I wish I could say I used a sledge hammer or something, but all I had was a can of red spray paint."

During the spell of silence that followed, the custody sergeant showed up, and the two men were escorted to a processing room, where Vanderlay spotted a camera mounted on the ceiling. The worrying possibility of incriminating video footage showing up on YouTube led him to conclude that keeping a low profile was the best course of action.

A cop sitting at a desk looked up from his computer and addressed HD. "Aren't you a piece of work," he said. "No fixed address, no ID, and no proper name."

HD shrugged. "I'm an anomaly, I know."

When the formalities of the printing process were complete, they were taken back to their cell.

Vanderlay examined the tips of his ink-smudged fingers. "I can't believe this is happening. I've never been arrested before."

"You're in good company," HD replied. "Gandhi and Mandela spent time in jail, too."

Aria arrived at her building, nodded to the security guy in the lobby, and made her way up to the second floor. The cacophonous thrum of a band rehearsing in one of the units greeted her as she stepped into the hall. Down the corridor, each apartment offered its own dramatic soundtrack—more music, a dog barking, someone crying. She arrived at her door feeling like she had run the gauntlet. She closed the door and then stood there for a moment, breathing in the relative quiet of the room, a reprieve that lasted until she reached for the light switch. As it clicked uselessly in the dark, her thoughts moved to the ice cream in the freezer, the milk and raita in the fridge—the things that would spoil without power. A moment later she was fumbling blindly through a drawer in one of the antique end tables stacked next to the entrance. The flashlight wasn't there, but she did find a candle and a pack of matches.

In a circle of flickering light she made her way to the fusebox. She had just pulled the panel door open, when her attention was drawn to the empty space on the counter where the machine should have been. Beyond that the curtains on the fire escape window were being gently blown by a breeze coming in through what she could see was a broken pane of glass. It was then that she noticed that the alley itself was awash in a series of chaotically flashing lights. With her heart pounding in her chest, she pulled her phone out of her pocket and called 9-1-1. She had just relayed her address, when the light in the alley way grew more intense. She backed away, instinctively retreating to the nearest door. She slammed it closed behind her with a force that momentarily delayed the realization that she had just locked herself in the bathroom.

She could think of nothing worse than ending up like Oliver Silverman—a delusional fool relegated to a self-imposed prison with a dozen fans blowing her preposterous thoughts about the room, and yet, there she was recalling what he had said about aliens using your phone to track you. And then she remembered something else he had said about there being no documented cases of someone being abducted while swimming. The next thing she knew she was standing in the tub with the faucet running. As the water rose around her ankles she was struck by another horrible thought—somewhere in the day's travels she had also lost the Boulangeot.

She let the weight of this realization pull her down into the tub. As the cold water soaked into her clothes, she began counting backwards from seven, picturing each number, inhaling, exhaling, sinking, surfacing. Seven dwarves, seven deadly sins, seven wonders of the world, seven compositions. Beethoven, *String Quartet in B-flat*, six degrees of separation, six feet under. Each time she inhaled her chest broke the surface, and then she went under again. Five fingers, five golden rings, Beethoven's *Fifth Symphony*, the five aspects of Vishnu, the fifth estate—panchama avastha. Four seasons, four and twenty blackbirds, four horsemen, Bach's *The Well-tempered Clavier Prelude in C*. As she sank again, she longed to stay there, like a stone, something that would not be missed or resuscitated. Three blind mice, Mozart's *The Magic Flute*, Tea for Two, Brandenburg Concerto No. 2 in F. One is the loneliest number, a single drop of rain, Stravinsky's *Rite of Spring*, a solitary note. Eka, the one cosmic soul—Hiranyagarbha. She took a deep breath, exhaled and went under. Zero. Oblivion.

The concert Vincent had attended earlier that evening was a disaster. He couldn't stop thinking about how foolish he had been to lend Aria the Boulangeot. The worry had gotten so bad that halfway through the final movement of Mendelssohn's *Piano Concerto No. 1, Op. 25*, he rose from his seat and excused his way to the aisle. As soon as he was out of the auditorium, he hurried into the washroom where he stationed himself in front of a sink. He looked in the mirror and saw a subtle twitch in his left eye. Something drastic had to be done. "I made a mistake and now I've got to fix it," he said to himself. As he dried his hands he came up with the plan to get Aria's address from the Finn and Clay computer, go to her residence, and insist on the violin's return. He shoved the bathroom door open and marched across the foyer.

Through the rain-streaked glass he could see debris blown by the wet wind across the parking lot. A siren echoed off the wall of the church down the street. "You can do this," he said as he stepped out into the storm. "You have no choice."

By the time he had arrived at Aria's building, he was having second thoughts about confronting her unannounced. Another pep talk got him to the lobby door, where he had to loiter by the bike rack until someone jumped out of a cab and hurried up the walkway to the entrance. Vincent said hello and followed the person in. As they walked by the security booth, he stayed close enough that it looked like they were together. He then double-checked the apartment number and climbed the stairs to the second floor.

The walls were rumbling with subwoofer explosions from a video game, the thud and crash of a badly played rendition of "Stairway to Heaven". When he got to Aria's apartment the entrance was covered in yellow police tape. He hurried back to the apartment where the band was rehearsing and knocked as loudly as he could. The music stopped, and, after a long pause, he heard the floor creak on the other side of the door.

"Who is it?"

"I'm a friend of Aria's in apartment 203," he said.

A kid with long blonde hair appeared with what Vincent could see was a very nice Les Paul hanging low on his hip.

"I was just wondering if you know what's going on," Vincent said, gesturing to Aria's door.

The kid stuck his head out in the hall. "Yeah, yeah, all kinds of crazy shit went down."

"Crazy shit?"

"Yeah, the fire department were the first to arrive."

"The fire department?"

"Yeah, they kicked the door open. Then the cops showed up. Then the ambulance."

Vincent placed a hand on the doorframe to steady himself.

"I don't know exactly what happened, but as far as I could make out, the lady drowned in the bathtub, but then the paramedics revived her and took her to the hospital."

As the final gusts of the chaotic day shoved Bailey toward home, she checked her social media. The dog photo now had a hundred and forty-two hearts, which was an all time high for her animal posts. She was about to check the comments when her phone rang. It was her grandmother's number. Something terrible must have happened. Why else would she be calling so late?

"Hi, Nani," she said as brightly as she could manage. "Is everything okay?"

"Hello sweetheart. I hope I didn't wake you."

"I'm up," she said. "I've been putting in some extra hours."

"Everybody is so busy these days. In fact, that's why I'm calling. I can't reach your mom or dad."

Bailey began to relax. "I haven't heard from them," she said, skirting around a group of girls who had just stumbled out of a club, "but I wouldn't worry. Dad is probably at work, and Mom, well, she's probably on a plane to Greenland or something."

"She's gone to Greenland?"

"No, I just mean, you just never know with her. I'm sure they're both—"

"Why is it so loud?" her grandmother interrupted.

"It's Friday night. People are out."

"You're out at this time of night?"

"Yes, I—"

"I want you to head home right away."

Bailey rolled her eyes. "Nani, I'm fine."

"It's not safe. There are tigers on the loose."

"Tigers? What are you talking about?"

"Just get home. And tell your father—if you hear from him—to call me. It's important. And don't forget the sraddha on Sunday."

Bailey dropped her phone back in her purse. Her whole family had gone completely crazy. Her father was sleeping on the floor of an empty house, and her mother, well, Bailey couldn't forget the day she had shown up unannounced at her studio to find her mother frantically securing a sleeping bag to a backpack. When Bailey saw the airline ticket to Kabul on the counter, she felt as if she had been punched in the heart. "You're going to Afghanistan?"

"I don't really have time to explain it," she said, grabbing the ticket, "but I love you—that's the most important thing—I love you, and I'm sorry."

As her mother dragged the backpack toward the door, Bailey panicked. "What in the world is going on?" she said.

"I know it's crazy, but I keep having these dreams about Dhani. He's alone. In a hole of some kind. But, well, he's alive."

Bailey called her father. "You need to come to Mom's right now," she told him.

"I'm at work," he said. "What's going on?"

"Dad, please don't—" She heard her mother opening the door. "Never mind, it's too late. Meet me at the airport. International departures. Please, Dad, this is no joke."

They were standing in line at the luggage check-in when her father arrived. Bailey waved him over, but he stopped next to a car rental kiosk to answer his phone. She stepped under the strip of nylon that corralled the zigzagging line of travellers and ran over to him.

He raised a finger in the air. "One sec," he said and turned away from her.

Bailey looked at her mother. The line was moving faster now.

"Okay," her father said, "I'll be there as soon as I can." He then tucked his phone into his pocket. "Sorry," he said.

Bailey was relieved by the agitation in his voice. It meant that he was actually an ally.

"She's lost it, Dad. She's flying to Kabul."

He stood there a moment with a blank look on his face.

"You have to stop her," she added. "She thinks Dhani is still..."

He took a step forward, then stopped. "It's too late," he said.

When she turned around, her mother, who now had her boarding pass, waved and then passed through the gate.

Bailey could feel something in her core—her soul, if she had such a thing—harden into the shape of her fist.

By the time she arrived at her apartment she was soaking wet and angry all over again. She made her way up the stairs, unlocked the door, and kicked off her wet boots. As soon as she clicked on a light, she was greeted by the chatter of the various creatures she had adopted, excitedly scurrying about in their cages. After checking to make sure each animal's water dish was full, she poured herself a glass of wine and headed to the bathroom. Just as she was about to step into the tub, she remembered that she had called Noah.

Woken by a crack of thunder, Vanya sat up in the dark and rested her head against the wall. The rain and wind, loud against the bedroom window, were accompanied by a chorus of noises from within the house. After identifying the source of each sound—the *tick-tock* of the clock on the dresser, the far-off hum of the fridge, a creak in the joists—she sat there for another long moment, wondering if she had the courage or the strength to deal with what was coming. A second strike of lightning lit up the room, and in that brief instant she saw that Annu had pulled the covers up over his head. "Not again," she whispered.

This latest development in Annu's withdrawal was worrying, if not that surprising. His idiosyncratic moods had always been connected to the weather. He even believed that his successes and failures as a violinist had as much to do with meteorology as with technique and talent—the temperature outside and the geothermal conditions inside the auditorium all played a part. "A concert in winter in New Delhi," he once told her, "will be notably distinct from a summer show in Kerala." It was, in fact, Annu's sensitivities regarding the weather that led to the premature end of his career.

His final performance had taken place on an unusually mild December evening. Annu had noted that the air pressure and humidity were optimal, but a cold front was moving in. To stay ahead of the coming storm, he played right through the intermission. Vanya never forgot just how rapturous that performance was. After striking the final note, he raised his violin in one hand, the bow in the other, and stood there in an apparent state of exalted bliss. The audience rose to their feet in an exuberant ovation. Annu did not bow or open his eyes. The clapping stopped, and still he stood there centre stage with his arms extended. By the time Annu opened his eyes, with the exception of Vanya and Aria in the twelfth row, the auditorium was empty.

Later in the dressing room he told her that the audience had missed it—that they had left before the last note had utterly and completely vanished.

When the temperature dropped below zero, he cancelled the remaining two shows on the tour. His agent criticized him for his eccentricity, and to make matters worse, a column in the Arts section of the *Globe* claimed that, while deeply impassioned and technically exquisite, his variations and interpretations were outdated and romantic. He went to bed that night, pulled the covers over his head, and spent the next three days repeating the Lakshmi Gayatri Sloka, reaching a pale thin arm out from the covers to take a bowl of dhal or a cup of tea before retreating back into his fortress of prayer.

Vanya knew this business with the bedcovers was his way of trying to reduce the world to a manageable size, to recalibrate and make whatever adjustments were necessary to repair the damage inflicted on his heart. But it was also a sign that her own ability to control things was waning. Her husband was losing his faculties. There were tigers on the loose in the city. The foundation of devotion and prayer that she had maintained for so many years was no longer enough.

364 days after Dhani's death

Time is moving at a stutter, accelerating, slowing down. You hear the thud of something hitting the floor in another room. Doors complain as they open, cracks form in the ceiling, the space between things tightens, the pressure causes the load-bearing struts to vibrate. There is nothing but you to hold it all up, every minute, every second, holding. When you step outside, even the sky seems compromised, another unstable threat. You are no longer sure about what can be trusted, the world has become a dream, a construct, a poem of sadness. Unannounced, always unannounced, the hurt rumbles across your mind and quakes in your chest. All your efforts of distraction lead you back to a time before, a reprisal of those countless nights coming in late from work, your children dreaming in their beds. Do not disturb this peace, this contract with the sleeping. Be quiet, and close the cupboard door softly. Be sure to make as little noise as possible when you carry a plate of cheese and olives into the living room to watch the television with the volume turned off. But even this memory is cluttered with noise, with the sound of invisible hammers hitting invisible rocks. The clang and thud of hard labour. It is just a matter of time before the whole thing crumbles.

Six

Vanderlay's mind kept returning to the moment the soldiers arrived at his door. The budgie whistled, the doorbell rang, and the knot tightened in his stomach. He knew that the discomfort in his gut had always been there, but now it had grown into the anxious need to be somewhere, anywhere other than where he was. He paced the cell, ten strides from one wall to the other, turn and repeat, until he eventually collapsed onto the filthy floor, pulled his legs up to his chin, and tried to steer his mind toward a memory dramatic and painful enough to distract him. He revisited the day Bailey broke her arm, the time Dhani almost drowned at a friend's cottage, his own motorcycle accident. When he felt the approach of another wave of anxiety, he took a long breath and pushed further into the shadows. In this darkness, he felt the temperature drop, his bare feet touching down on the cold floor of his childhood bedroom. He followed the memory into the dim hallway, past the spare room where his grandmother was sleeping, the bathroom, and then on into the living room where he could see the frost that had formed in the corners of each pane of glass in the bay window. He knew the dendritic structures had something to do with water vapour and the cold outside, but he wasn't sure how or why the intricate crystals spiked out into such beautiful feathery shapes. He was about to wipe at the fogged glass with the sleeve of his pyjamas when the phone began to ring. He hurried to answer it before it woke his grandmother. The caller identified themselves as a representative of an airline insurance company and then, in a measured tone, told Vanderlay that his parents were listed as passengers on Flight 195 en route to Cancun. "Due to a malfunctioning Fuel Quantity Information System Processor the aircraft did not reach its destination. There were no survivors." Vanderlay felt something clench his fourteen-year-old heart until each excruciating beat left him wishing he could somehow vacate his own body, claw his way out of his skin.

When HD slumped forward on the bench, Vanderlay was brought sharply back to the cell. He reflexively assessed HD's body language: the irregularity of his breath, the pallor of his skin, then took a knee and placed his fingers on HD's pulse. "Are you okay?" he asked.

HD was non-responsive for a second before he spoke. "It's nothing," he said. "It'll pass."

Vanderlay was relieved to see that there was no ptosis or abnormal eye movement. "Any pain or numbness?" he asked

"No."

"Dizziness? Vision problems?"

"Dizziness," HD offered reluctantly.

"I'd like you to raise both arms above your head?"

Suddenly HD's eyes cleared, and he straightened himself up. "You some kind of a doctor?" he asked. "Or just someone who can't mind their own business?"

"I am," Vanderlay said, "guilty of the former and the latter."

HD gave his head a shake, "It's just a palpitation." He then took a deep breath and positioned himself in a kind of sideways yoga posture. "I appreciate the concern," he added, "but I promise you, I have no intention of dying in a jail cell."

Could just be dehydration, Vanderlay thought. "When's the last time you had a physical?"

"A physical?" HD asked. A wheezing cough interrupted the laugh that followed.

"I know it's complicated being homeless," Vanderlay said, "but you should pop in to a walk-in clinic for a check-up every six months. It's mandatory for someone of your age."

HD smiled and then sat up straight. "I know it may be difficult for you to understand this," he said, "but it's not complicated at all. I'm simply a man who prefers a peripatetic, debt-free lifestyle, and as such, I don't march to the beat of the same drum as you."

Vanderlay was relieved to see that HD's breathing was returning to normal, but he wanted to keep him talking, both to be sure the old man was stable and to keep his own mind occupied. "One of those minimalists, are you?" He moved back across the cell to continue his observations from the far wall.

"Look, " HD said, "the real difference between you and me is that my day-to-day choices are influenced by what I need—food, clothing, water, the means by which I get from point A to B, while your choices are motivated by what you *want*—higher education, the latest this and that in modern technology, quality footwear. We're both just acting in service of our highest priorities. Priorities that shape our perspectives. Perspectives that define what we choose to see, and what we willfully dismiss."

Vanderlay let himself slide back to the floor. The idea of priorities and perspectives struck him as something he needed to address. "My highest priority," he said, "is to be a good doctor—a good husband and father." He had the sense that he only had a few more seconds to express something crucial before it was gone. "The truth is, I've been performing rather poorly on all three fronts, but failing as a parent is the hardest to reconcile." Vanderlay tucked his trembling hands into his armpits. "My daughter hasn't said more than three words to me in the last three months, and my son, well... When he chose to join the military I didn't even try to talk him out of it. I wanted to. I mean, it was probably the last thing on earth I wanted him to do, but I just couldn't stand in the way of something he seemed so passionate about." Vanderlay could feel the floor vibrating through the soles of his feet. Hold it together, he told himself. But at that moment he no longer wanted to. "My son was lost, confused, and scared. And what did I do? I told him that he should follow his heart. Wherever that may take him." Vanderlay closed his eyes. "As a doctor I have lost count of the number of lives I have saved, but I couldn't save my own son."

When he felt HD's hand on his shoulder, his impulse was to shrug it off, but there was something so comforting in the gentle pressure and weight of it, something totally unconditional.

"I'm sorry," he said, "the thorny trick of accepting comfort from others is something I'm really not very good at."

❧

It was just getting light when Vanderlay, HD, and four other men were ushered into another police transport vehicle. Vanderlay noted how the night in jail seemed to have taken something from each of them. The guy directly across from Vanderlay was the exception. He appeared to be in a meditative trance.

Vanderlay wrapped his arms around his chest and tried to warm himself against the chills running through his bones. When he looked over at HD, he heard a slight asthmatic wheeze in his breath. "How are you feeling?" he asked.

"Tired as hell," HD said, "but I'm looking forward to getting this mishap over with—get myself back on the road."

Vanderlay nodded and closed his eyes.

"Are you okay?" HD asked.

"Everyone keeps telling me I need a holiday," Vanderlay responded. "I'm beginning to think they might be right."

"Or maybe you need something more substantial. Something like actual change."

"You saying I should quit my job and become a hobo?"

"I would never presume to tell a man what he should do with his life, but I think it's worth pointing out that a gilded cage is still a cage."

"What does that mean?"

HD moved his feet a couple inches further apart, as if what he was about to say required a more firm footing. "I'm guessing an educated man like yourself has read Thoreau."

"I can't say I have," Vanderlay replied.

"*Walden*," HD said, "documents the two years that Thoreau spent in the Concord woods where he built a cabin, grew food, fished, and studied the natural world around him." He paused and took a long, deep breath. "I mention it because, at its heart, it's a philosophical treatise on authenticity, intuition, and living with integrity. It's one of the most sobering things I've ever read. Taught me how to see things for what they are, not what I wanted them to be."

"But running off to the woods and leaving everything behind—isn't that just a form of escapism?"

The guy who had been meditating started banging the back of his head rhythmically on the wall of the van.

HD pointed a finger. "That is escapism," he said. "In fact, working too much, reaching for your phone every two minutes, binging on television—most people are in a constant state of escapism, whether they know it or not."

Vanderlay's impulse was to get up and rouse the young man banging his head from his trance, both to stop him from potentially injuring himself and to put an end to the noise.

"Thoreau," HD continued, "wasn't running away; he was trying to confront life in its simplest form. He believed that the daily communion with nature would lead to a more authentic existence."

Vanderlay sighed. "To be honest, I can't say I know what living an authentic existence even means."

"Well, I think it has to do with being conscious of the choices we make. Engaging with the world in ways that are responsible, in harmony, so to speak, with nature, but just as importantly, in ways that make us feel connected."

Once again Vanderlay had the sense that time was running out, that if he didn't articulate what he was feeling in that moment, he never would. "I've been living with a sense of impending doom since I was fourteen years old. It's there when I look up at the sky. It's there in the tectonic plates. It's there in the vulnerability of the heart. I went to med school to prove that, given a chance, death could be—"

Just then, the van lurched and went into a skid. As the six men slid toward the front of the vehicle, shoes squeaked across the metal floor, shoulders slammed into cheekbones. And then, as the van came to an abrupt stop, the lot of them were thrown with equal force in the opposite direction, the chaos settling into a calm and still silence.

Vanderlay opened his eyes and found himself pressed against the back window. Outside, in the early-morning rain, people were getting out of their vehicles and approaching the van. He was just about to turn and see if HD was okay, when he saw a striped haunch, two padded feet, and a long orange and black tail protruding from under the back bumper.

❧

When Aria woke, all that she could see were dark and vague shapes—a window to her right, a door to the left. A moment later the blurred outline of a wheelchair and an IV pole came into view. As each object seemed to swell and recede before her, she noticed that someone was in the room with her. She was trying desperately to focus, when a flash of lightning drew her attention to the window. Rain was inexplicably falling several metres away from the glass, as if something really big was hovering over the building.

❧

Vincent pushed the wheelchair over to the side of the bed and took a seat. Despite the low light, he could see that Aria was in bad shape, and even still, she was beautiful. He leaned in until he was close enough to smell the fragrance of her hair. Blood orange or mandarin, he guessed. "Please," he whispered, "where is the violin?"

She opened her eyes. Her dilated pupils had all but obliterated her irises. "There," she said, pointing at the ceiling, "on the roof."

She closed her eyes again. He reached out to rouse her, but as soon as his hand touched hers, an electric charge arced through his fingers, ran up his arms, and then ricocheted around in his skull, leaving him with the idea, absurd as it was, that she was telling him how the violin was on the hospital roof. A moment or two later, he was wearing a lab coat and a pair of yellow cleaning gloves, which helped vitiate the electric shocks as he hoisted Aria out of the bed. Once she was in the chair, he pushed her out of the room, slipped past the nurses' station without detection, and then boarded an elevator. Each time the doors opened, Vincent busied himself with what he imagined were doctorly activities. By the time the elevator arrived at the top floor, he was nervously whistling what to his embarrassment turned out to be the theme to *Sesame Street.*

When the doors finally closed behind him, he steered the wheelchair down the corridor until he came to a sign that said, *Exit to Roof. Authorized Personnel Only.* A little shove with the sole of his tasseled loafer and the door swung open.

He positioned himself in front of the wheelchair. The heavy rain, a discordant concert of flashing lights, and the uneven surface of gravel pitching toward the edge of the building inspired a woozy fit.

Though Aria's eyes were open again, it was clear she was not fully conscious.

"Okay," he said. "where is—"

The pupils in Aria's eyes, now large circles of impenetrable blackness, were fixed on something behind him.

"Don't look, whatever you do," he whispered to himself.

He turned and looked. The anxiety was so overwhelming that he retreated to his "safe place," where he imagined his fingers on the keys of the pearl-white Bosendorfer Imperial Concert Grand, playing a Franz Liszt concerto, the melody of which usually elicited visions of pastoral tranquility, gambolling lambs in a field of yellow daisies. But now, the piano keys were too far apart, the seat was too low. Unable to reach the pedals or the notes that made up each chord, he panicked all over again. This time, he ran.

Bailey awoke with a splitting headache and the vague memory of a dream about her brother and the missing dog. As she was getting up she caught her reflection in the mirrored vanity. "No, no, no," she whispered. She looked over at Noah's stubbly face mashed into the pillow next to her. He grunted and flopped over so that the scabby dragon tattoo on his shoulder was visible. She remembered him showing her the tattoo the night before. "I was born in the year of the dragon," he had told her, as he flexed his shoulder muscles. Bailey felt a wave of dry regret rush up from her stomach. According to the placemats at a Chinese restaurant her family went to a few months back, her father was a dragon as well, which of course meant that Noah and her father were probably the same age.

She hurried into the bathroom where she grabbed a bottle of Aspirin out of the cabinet. The pills scratched at her throat as they went down. When she confronted herself in the mirror, she saw that the bruise under her eye was now purple and yellow. The rest of her face looked slightly blurred—confirmation that she was in fact disappearing. At that moment, the idea of vanishing from the face of the earth didn't seem like such a bad thing.

The ache and regret followed her into the kitchen, where she dragged a flat of containers out of the cupboard: premium cat food, organic blend guinea pig chow, rabbit pellets, hamster seed, ferret protein mix, and a jar of iguana food. As she tiptoed through the apartment filling bowls, trays, and water dishes, she found herself wishing that all the animals she had adopted would vanish along with her. Let's just get this over with, she thought. This slow erasing of her existence was becoming unbearable.

After finishing her rounds she took out her phone to check the time. When she saw that it was 4 am she wasn't sure what to do. There was no going back to bed, and she dreaded the idea of dealing with Noah. She scrolled down to his number, typed two words and hit send.

She went to the coffee table and gathered the missing dog posters. Looks like I have to do this alone after all, she told herself.

She had just pulled a hoodie over her head when there, outside the window, alone in the middle of the dark wet street, the dog appeared.

She ran for the door, but by the time she got down the stairs, it was already gone.

Vanya wasn't sure how long she had been standing there in front of the bathroom mirror, but as her reflection began to shift and distort into the folded layers of gloom, it felt as if the room itself had somehow become disconnected from the house and was hovering in a sleep-suspended drift. As she continued to stare into the mirror's depths, the vaguely distorted shape of Annu appeared. He was wearing the suit he used to wear when he played at the train station back home, forty years ago—single button with a notched satin collar, an ivory shirt with pin-tuck pleats, a bow tie, and a top hat. As she placed her hands on the sink and leaned in, she saw that he was standing on the platform of what looked like a subway station.

After tuning the instrument he removed the hat he was wearing and placed it on the floor in front of him. When he plucked one of the strings, the hat began to vibrate. A moment later, a low and throaty growl rose into the surrounding darkness. Another string was plucked, and the hat began to shake and contort with a violence that suggested something was struggling to get out. A third note was struck, and a paw appeared, and then another. The top hat continued to swell and strain until a whiskered snout emerged from the hat's impossible depths. As Annu drew the bow across a string, a vaudevillian vibrato accentuated the trick until the tiger was shaking what was left of the shredded hat from the end of its tail. When it turned its wild and predatory gaze toward the source of the music, Vanya turned to the wall and flicked on the light.

As the trick of the mirror gave way once again to her own reflection, she was struck by just how haggard she looked. The lines on her face were deeper, her eyes hardened with worry. The wear and tear, she thought, of forty-odd years bearing this inherited burden.

Seven

As soon as Vanderlay stepped out of the courthouse, he felt the weight of the outside world there waiting for him. He stood there a second, letting the concerns of this new day settle, and then checked his phone—he still had an hour before his shift started at the hospital, but there were six missed calls. He was just about to check his messages, when he spotted HD in front of the cenotaph, fussing with a piece of gear strapped to a backpack.

It took more effort than he expected to move his legs. "Hey," he called out, "I figured you'd be long gone by now."

HD smiled. "I thought I'd wait around to say a proper goodbye."

Vanderlay took a deep breath. "I'm glad you did. I wanted to thank you for the company. I imagine I could have done a lot worse in the cellmate department."

"Feeling's mutual," HD said. "How's your head?"

Vanderlay touched the abrasion just below his hairline. "Bit of a headache, but I'm fine. I still can't believe we ran over a ti"—he paused to check his ringing phone. "My wife's real estate agent," he said as he declined the call. "She wants to have the house appraised." He smiled awkwardly. "Sorry. Been free for all of five minutes, and already checked my phone twice." It rang again.

HD grabbed the straps of his pack, "Well, I won't keep you," he said. He was about to haul his gear onto his shoulders, when he saw that Vanderlay was staring up at the sky. He let the weight settle back on the cement. "I know I keep asking you this, but are you sure you're okay?"

"I can't shake this feeling," Vanderlay said. "I just got out of jail, and yet I don't feel free at all. In a strange way, I actually felt more relaxed—" He was looking up at the sky again.

HD unzipped a pouch in the top of his pack and pulled out a book. "Hold on a second," he said. When he got to a page marked with a wooden matchstick, he ran a finger halfway down the first paragraph. "Here we are—*I was put into a jail once for one night,*" HD's voice was calm and authoritative—"*and as I stood considering the walls of solid stone, the door of wood and iron a foot thick and the iron grating which strained the light, I could not help think of the foolishness of that institution which treated me as if I were mere flesh and blood and bones to be locked up... I did not for a moment feel confined and the walls seemed to be a great waste of stone and mortar. In every threat and in every compliment there was a blunder: for they thought my chief desire was to stand on the other side of that stone wall. I could not but smile to see how industriously they locked the door on my meditations, which followed them out again without let or hindrance...*"

"Thoreau?"

HD nodded.

"I'm not sure I can appreciate exactly what all that means."

"I think what he's saying is that prison is a state of mind."

He handed Vanderlay the book and then grabbed his gear again. Once the pack was on his back, he took hold of the straps and adjusted the weight on his shoulders. "I'd go as far as to say, there's more than one kind of prison. Houses, jobs, technology... Sometimes the things we own become the things that own us."

"I guess I have some re-evaluating to do."

When Vanderlay realized he was still holding the book, he offered it back to HD. "Don't forget this."

"I don't need it anymore," HD replied. "I'm going to the source."

"You're going to Walden?"

"Last stop on my bucket list."

Vanderlay reached for his wallet. "Let me give you some money then. It's the least I can do."

"You still don't get it, do you?"

"I guess I don't."

"I'm not destitute. In fact, in some ways, I'm much richer than you are."

Vanderlay looked down at his wallet. "There are things we need, and there are things we want."

"Now you're on the right track."

"Well," Vanderlay said, handing HD a business card. "If you ever need a billboard vandalized, give me a call."

"And if you ever get around to taking that holiday, you know where to find me."

Vanderlay watched HD shuffle down the steps, then tucked the book into the pocket of his jacket. "You should get your heart looked at," he said.

The old man turned. "Funny, I was going to say the same thing to you."

As Noah pulled on his pants, his phone fell out of his back pocket. When he picked it up he saw the message from Bailey and sat back down on the bed to read it. He initially thought the text, *It's lover*, was some kind of romantic declaration, but then he realized her finger had accidentally dragged over the "l" on its way to the "o". I've been such an idiot, he thought. Caught in the spell of a teenage girl.

He got up and headed for the bedroom door. Just say good morning, he told himself, act like you haven't seen the message and tell her you have to go.

When he discovered that he was alone in the apartment, he stopped in the living room and took stock. He knew he was the bad guy in this, and yet, he felt as if he was the one who was being hurt. He turned in a slow circle, and as he took inventory of the creatures rustling in the various enclosures stacked against the living room wall, he was suddenly inspired with a righteous sense of purpose.

During the hour it took to load the cages into the van, he kept telling himself that returning all these animals to the shelter was the right thing to do. But as soon as he climbed in behind the wheel, the heavy rain on the roof sounded like the vehicle was being pelted with accusing stones. He sat there staring out the windshield, his mind spiralling back to the night before. The unexpected phone call, the sound of Bailey's distressed voice, his promise to swing by and help in any way he could, the excitement and hesitation as he drove to her apartment. When she answered the door holding a cat and a ferret in her arms, while at the same time keeping a plump white rabbit from escaping into the hall with her foot, the excitement turned to curiosity. He followed her into the living room, lit by a single lamp on the floor. In that low light he saw a dozen or so cages stacked under the window. The place smelled like cat litter with a hint of strawberries. "Wow," he said, eyeing a guinea pig that was chewing on an extension cord, "it's a zoo in here."

Bailey let the cat drop to the floor and then placed the ferret on the couch next to a pair of purple socks, and what Noah guessed was a napping chuckwallas iguana.

"I know," she said. "I've bit off more than I can chew."

"You know, a lost dog may be the least of your—" When he saw that she might start crying, he changed directions. "Never mind all that," he said, "I told you I was going to help, and that's what I'm here to do."

He watched her slide down onto the floor in front of the coffee table, move a pile of dirty dishes out of the way, and then reach for a stack of paper. The words *Missing Dog* were written above a black and white printout of the photo she had taken earlier that day at the shelter.

"Okay," she said tearing between the phone numbers printed vertically across the bottom. "I've got fifty of these. Once we get them done, we can poster the city."

She picked up a mug and took a sip of something that made her red lips glisten. His eyes went to an empty bottle he spotted on the cluttered coffee table. "I see you like French," he said, examining the label. "I prefer something more robust, like a Rioja, but a Merlot pairs nicely with a search and rescue mission."

To his surprise, Bailey got up and headed for the kitchen.

As he returned the empty bottle to the table, a distorted glimpse of his desire provoked an inconvenient moment of introspection during which he found himself both eyeing the door and wondering what Bailey would look like naked. Before he could decide what to do, she returned with a bottle of something cheap and Canadian, handed him a glass, and sat back down. Next thing he knew, he was sitting on the floor beside her.

By the second pour of wine, the little slur in her voice confirmed that the empty bottle he had examined had been consumed before he arrived. By the third pour, he was inserting playful and flirtatious banter into the conversation. By the fourth, he was massaging her bare feet. By the fifth glass, they were in the bedroom where she blew a kiss to a cage of white mice, paused to speak a little gibberish to a hedgehog, and then, in the dim light, as Noah was about to undo her bra, she ran to the bathroom and threw up in the toilet.

When Noah returned to the present moment, he was stopped at a red light several blocks from Bailey's apartment. He lit a cigarette, rolled down the window, and tossed the match out onto the road. As he exhaled a lung full of smoke, something caught his eye in the side mirror. It took a second to be sure because of the rain, but there was no mistaking the markings and the awkward gait. He took a cellphone photo of the dog with the ratty pink leash dragging behind, clicked on the share button, typed in Bailey's number, and hit send.

❧

After an hour spent taping her posters to lamp posts and bus shelters, Bailey stopped at a doughnut shop for a much needed reprieve from the rain. She sat there sipping her coffee, wallowing in the fact that her miserable life now included a regrettable one night stand. She shoved her mug off the edge of the table, took a photo, and posted it. #brokenhearted #caffeinebuzz #catharsis #nevergiveup.

The next hour was spent popping into boutique pet supply stores and vet clinics, asking if she could put up a poster in their windows. When she came upon a small crowd gathered under the marquee of the Royal Alexandra Theatre, she held up her phone displaying the picture of the dog and asked if anyone had seen it. An old lady with a red umbrella leaned in for a better look. "Oh, yes," she said, "he does look familiar."

Bailey felt a warm surge of optimism envelope her heart.

"That's the dog from that old record label."

The brief glimmer of hope evaporated. Bailey felt the wet cement penetrating the bottom of her boots water-log her socks and then seep into the soles of her feet. She began to shiver, and as the cold rain continued, her knees bloated, her hips swelled, and pearls of excess water began to drip from her finger tips. Just as the rising water began to slosh around inside of her skull, her phone vibrated, and Noah's photo of the dog appeared on the screen.

❧

Aria awoke just as the nurse arrived with breakfast. She watched him place the tray on the bedside table and then head over to the window and open the blinds. When he turned to see her watching, a look of concern crossed his face.

"Good to see you're awake," he said. "You had quite the night."

A series of fragmented images flashed through Aria's mind—something about being engulfed in a cacophony of light and noise. She could feel the panic and stress still there in her body.

When the nurse started asking her questions, it became clear that there were swaths of time that she could not recall.

"Well, it's a good thing we found you," he said. "I can't tell you how dangerous it is up there next to the medical transport site with all those helicopters coming and going."

"Helicopters?" The idea that there was a rational explanation for the chaos she was recalling struck Aria as a great relief.

"When can I get out of here?" she asked.

"Someone will be coming in to do an assessment this afternoon. In the meantime, you need rest."

The nurse checked her blood pressure and temperature, made some notes on the chart, then left the room.

Aria stared at the scrambled eggs and cold toast. She found herself thinking of somewhere tropical and warm. Somewhere with ancient ruins and jungle wildlife. Somewhere rare and exciting enough to distract her from—it struck her that she had spent the last twenty years travelling to escape the things she just couldn't bring herself to face. Whether it was an archeological dig in Syria or a hot air balloon ride across the Serengeti, it amounted to the same thing. The same was truc for Vanderlay, who had his own ways of avoiding life. His inability to face his fear of flying was a case in point. The number of times he used his schedule to avoid a trip at the last minute was nothing short of agonizing. Even the kids knew what was going on. In fact, when Dhani was about fourteen, he told his father that the odds of a commercial airline crashing are like one in eleven million, and yet Vanderlay just couldn't bring himself to admit his fear.

Aria eased her legs over the side of the bed, checked her balance, then made her way to the cupboard. Her clothes were neatly stacked on a shelf along with her purse and phone. She sat back down on the bed, got dressed, and then called Vanderlay.

Eight

The names scratched into the side of the thirty-car freight HD was watching wheeze by reminded him that every person, every thing, had a story. His own name, scratched into the paint of more rail cars than he could remember, had become part of the tale these old trains had to tell. A life on the road had made him a witness to the secret life that took place in the ditches, under the bridges, and along the straight and narrow tracks that crossed the continent. At that moment, something about the rain and the smell of the rail yard had him reminiscing about the days of the old steam locomotives and fallen flags: the Chesapeake and Ohio, the Western Maryland, and the Pennsylvania Railroad—long-haul lines of boxcars as far as the eye could see. But the takeovers and the subsequent mergers and bankruptcies that followed reduced the Class 1 lines to a handful. It was mostly tankers and flat cars now that left him exposed to the elements, not to mention the rail bulls. Lately, he was more concerned about how much energy it took to simply climb aboard. Even a low-sided flatbed put a worrying strain on his heart.

Without knowing which side of the yard the east-bounders departed from, he decided to locate the switch crew. He knew the older employees were sometimes disgruntled enough that they didn't mind helping out a friendly traveller, so when he spotted a seasoned guy in a dirty pair of coveralls coming down the yard in an ATV, HD kicked at the loose gravel under his feet and took a tentative step. Rocks and stones skidded underfoot as he scuffed down the berm. On level ground, he recentred the weight of his pack, swatted at a few burrs clinging to his pants, and flagged the guy down. HD took note of the swollen hands, the dirt under his nails, the tools he was carrying, and then enquired about trains heading across the border. The brakeman pulled a radio from his belt, "I got a crazy old guy looking for an ETD on trains heading south."

A garbled response came back over the radio.

"We got a triple-eight-zero heading out to Jersey in about three minutes," the brakeman said. "It's a freight, six tracks over. Watch out for a white Ford pick-up. Inspector is a prick."

By the time HD made his way to the other side of the rail yard, his train—a long line of tankers with a few loaded flat beds at the end, was already moving. He normally wouldn't jump a haul like this one. Tankers sometimes carried toxic chemicals, and loaded flatcars could shift and either crush you or push you over the side. But today, the rain and lack of sleep conspired against his better judgment.

He was already breathing hard as he came up alongside a flat car. It was still moving slow, but it was loaded with six fifty-foot cylinders stacked three-two-one. He figured, once aboard, he could take his chances stowing himself inside one of the tubes, which would protect him from both the rain and security.

His first attempt to get his pack up on the flatcar was aborted when his knee clipped the tool box and threw him off stride. He had to reach down with one hand and make an adjustment to his gear as he ran. When he was parallel to the middle of the car, he reached for the thick strap holding the first row of cylinders, hoisted his pack up, and slid it onto the edge of the car bed. It was easier now to run, but he could feel his thighs ache as he struggled to keep pace with the accelerating train. "Okay, this is it," he told himself as the ladder on the flatcar approached from behind. He managed to get a good grip on the steel ring bolted to the car's floor, but the metal ladder's lowest step was two feet above the gravel, and when he aimed a foot at the first rung he didn't have the timing right. HD took three long awkward steps, but his fourth stride came up short, and he went down.

He skidded across the uneven gravel, sharp stones tearing at his elbows and knees. When he came to a halt on his gut, he instinctively rolled away from the train until he was lying flat on his back, the grind and clatter of the steel wheels slamming on the bucking track as it passed two feet away. He felt a radiating heat travel from his heart to his shoulders and then burn up into his temples. The last car rolled by and he knew his gear was lost—everything was lost.

While he lay there on the gravel assessing the damage, a crow perched on a switching light looked down at him and cawed into the drizzle. HD exhaled a high-pitched wheeze. He tried to raise his arms, but found that his left side was numb, which meant he could only examine the white and red meaty flesh exposed on his right hand. The crow alighted from its perch. Tears pooled in HD's eyes as he watched the bird circle above him. Another tear fell, and another crow appeared, and then another, and another. HD had experienced his share of strange things—fully coherent conversations with ghosts in empty boxcars, apparitions just below the surface of a frozen river. He had even seen an unidentified flying object in the night-time sky, beams of coloured lights scanning the ground. The mind concocts all manner of company to stave off the loneliness of travel. So it was no wonder that he was comforted by the sound of the birds' wings beating against the air as the sky blackened above him. He tried again to get up, but a knot of pain in his chest heeled him to the ground. When he closed his eyes, he felt the pull on his cardigan sleeves and trousers as the crows lifted him into the air. He imagined Thoreau—jotting notes in his field guide, sweeping the step of his cabin, hauling water up from the pond, surveying the land, concocting hexes against the progress of the surrounding towns. "Take me to Walden," he wanted to say, but when he opened his mouth all that could be heard was the dry whistle of a distant train.

The moment the hospital came into view, Vanderlay wondered if he was capable of managing the clinical exigencies of the ER. Each step he took was so hindered by the weight of his own body that it felt as though the earth's gravitation field had increased. He just need something to take the edge off. He entered the building through the concourse and then made his way down the hall past the chapel and the physio room. When he got to his office, he drew the blinds and took a seat at his desk. Valium or Ativan would do the job, he thought, as he unlocked the drawer. A second later he had a package of Adzenys in his shaking hands. He peeled back the blister wrap, but as he extracted one of the pills, his eyes fell on the family portrait sitting next to his computer monitor. He scratched at the stubble on his chin. The photo had been sitting there for the past two years, and yet, it wasn't until that moment that he saw how obviously his wife and kids were forcing themselves to smile. The look on his own face was equally troubling. It was the look of a man under duress, a look that would compel someone to ask if he was all right.

A sudden need to pinpoint the moment when the cracks first revealed themselves led to the memory of a late night conversation he'd had with Aria.

"I think we need to be spending more time with the kids," he had said.

Aria was in bed with the laptop. "What did you have in mind?"

"I was thinking of camping."

She started laughing. "Camping? Really?"

"Yes," he said, "unplug for a couple days. What do you think?"

Several seconds passed before his wife looked up from the laptop. "I'm sorry," she said, "I'm in a bidding war on eBay."

"That's exactly what I'm talking about. It's almost midnight, and the router is going crazy."

"Welcome to the twenty-first century" she said.

"I'm just saying that we could all benefit from a little break from all this streaming and texting and gaming and whatever."

When he climbed into bed, she leaned over and kissed him. "Maybe you're right," she said. "A family trip is a good idea."

It turned out Aria's idea of a family trip was a week at Disney World, which she pitched without consulting him at dinner the next day.

"Or," Vanderlay said as enthusiastically as he could, "we could all spend a few days in the great outdoors A good old fire, some fresh air, and a starry sky would be far more enriching than spending a week in a hotel."

"Disney World is much more than hotels and swimming pools," Aria said. She had her tablet open. "They have fireworks, live music, museums and restaurants, and some of the best roller coasters on the planet."

Looking around the table, it was clear that Bailey could barely contain herself, while Dhani wanted nothing to do with either idea.

In the end, they agreed that Vanderlay would take the kids camping and his wife would take them to Florida. She booked the flight and a hotel, made restaurant reservations, and bought tickets to Cirque du Soleil. The three of them came home tanned and satiated, and there were photos on Aria's phone of the three of them caught in what appeared to be genuine states of joy.

On the camping trip, which took place a few weeks later, a storm sent them into the tent at 7 pm on their first night. An hour and a half of card games by flashlight was enough to start the whining. By morning the tent was flooded, the firewood was wet, and the kids wanted to go home. As Vanderlay prepared breakfast on the portable stove, he wrote the trip off as a total failure. But then, as they all sat down together on a wet log to eat, Dhani revealed that his girlfriend had just broken up with him. Vanderlay wasn't even aware that his son had a girlfriend, but the look on his face made it clear that he was deeply hurt. At first he wasn't sure what to say. His feeling on the matter was that heartbreak was an inevitable part of life, a character builder—what doesn't kill you makes you stronger, and all that. While he was mulling this over, Bailey simply offered her brother the sympathy and support he needed. As the conversation between them continued, Vanderlay discovered that Dhani and the girl he was mourning had never actually been in the same room together. The year-long relationship had taken place via gaming and daily conversations on Discord. Once again, he didn't know what to say, but his son didn't pull away when he reached over and hugged him.

They packed up after breakfast, and as they piled into the car, Vanderlay amended the moratorium on cellphone use. The kids perked up immediately. Internet surfing and texting commenced. They spent the three-hour drive home in silence.

In the end, neither trip made a difference—a week later Dhani turned eighteen and joined the military.

When Vanderlay's phone started ringing, the room came back into focus.

"Hi," his wife said, "do you have a minute? I think we need to talk."

Their separation had come out of a prompt just like this. As the idea that she was now going to ask for a divorce took shape in his mind, he felt the room folding in on itself. He hung up, swallowed four pills, and got to his feet.

In the staff lounge, he gulped back a cup of coffee, made his way to the prep room, dawned his scrubs, and had a look at the patient tracker. There were several new arrivals, but they were all level 1 and 2. He was about to make his rounds, when it was announced that several critical patients were en route.

The moment he arrived at triage, a middle-aged man with a hemorrhaging shoulder wound was being lifted from the ambulance stretcher to the hospital gurney. The paramedic applying pressure to the patient's wound was tanned and had the look of someone who had recently been scuba diving on a coral reef.

"What do we got?" Vanderlay said.

"Dog or maybe a coyote attack," the paramedic replied. "He was hiking in the Don Valley. One bite, severe tissue trauma. He's lost a lot of blood."

The sheets around the wound were a deep vermilion red.

"Looks like the brachial artery may be severed. We need to get a clamp on it immediately," Vanderlay ordered.

At a closer look, he could see that the bite had left four distinct puncture wounds and that the top corner of the scapula had been shattered. "Not a dog or coyote," he said. "Something much bigger—" His mind flashed on the striped haunches of the thing the police van had run over earlier that morning. He wrote, *tiger bite?* on the chart and then took a deep breath.

"You okay?" the paramedic asked.

"I'm good," Vanderlay said. "Nothing a little holiday won't fix."

As the patient was wheeled off, the paramedic glanced back at Vanderlay. "Just got back from Cuba," he said. "Great beaches, and the local music is fantastic—highly recommended."

Vanderlay imagined himself strolling past the luggage check, through the security gate, the long corridor to the departure lounge, and then, just as he was stepping onto the boarding bridge the words *hit and run* drew his attention to the flashing lights at the emergency entrance.

A moment later he was standing over a thirty-year old female with glass shards in her hair, deep cuts around her eyes and nose. The nurses worked quickly, cutting the patient's clothing away. Vanderlay called out for the emergent imaging equipment to be brought bedside to scan for internal organ damage. "X-rays and CT scan," he added. "Looks like fractures in both legs, possible lateral compression in the pelvis area." He could feel himself easing into the rhythm, time blurring into a familiar procedural routine. I don't need a damn holiday, he thought. I just need to work harder. But when the next patient was wheeled in, Vanderlay felt a rush of adrenaline surge through his system.

"Oh Christ, no," he whispered. "I know this man."

"He was found unconscious," the attending paramedic said. "Asystolic and apneic."

Vanderlay noted the pale colour of his skin. Pulling back the eyelids, he aimed a flashlight at HD's pupils. Both were fixed and dilated. Eye, verbal, and motor responses were all absent. "Heart attack," he said. "I want oxygen, diamorphine, and glyceryl trinitrate, pronto." He then hastily opened the shirt to reveal a bypass scar running down the middle of a large eagle tattooed across HD's chest. Vanderlay ordered an echocardiograph and blood tests. Once the cardiac monitor was in place, the vitals were documented: blood pressure, heart rate, respiratory rate. A nurse intravenously administered the mixture of fluids, medications and blood product. A moment later, a ventilator breathing tube was placed down his throat.

"Doctor Stone," he heard someone call from behind. The light at the end of the hall silhouetted a waving flight attendant. "Buckle your seatbelt," she said. "We're about to take off."

Aria sat back on the hospital bed and called Vanderlay's number again. When it went to voicemail she left a message. "I don't know what just happened," she said, "but I called to say I'm sorry. I've been making a real mess of things, but it's clear to me now that—" the call timed out "—I don't want to do this alone anymore."

Out in the hall she shoved the empty wheelchair, marched past the nurse's station, and then stepped into an elevator. As the doors opened and closed in front of her, expecting mothers and people in various stages of recovery, some with terminal illnesses, entered and exited. She was reminded of Brahma, Vishnu, and Shiva, and how in this place the cycle of creation, preservation, and destruction were playing out on a daily basis.

She stepped out of the elevator in the lobby and hurried through the crowded concourse to the exit. It was still drizzling outside, but there was no longer a charge in the air, nothing hovering in the sky above. A cab pulling away from the curb reminded her that the last time she could remember having the Boulengeot in her possession was on the way to Oliver Silverman's.

When she googled the taxi company, she saw that the address was a few blocks down the street. She dialled the number and stepped out into the rain.

"Hello," a voice said, "Bluebird Taxi. How can I help you?"

"Hi," she said, "I'm trying to find a violin. I think I left it—"

"Hold please."

Several seconds passed during which she was subjected to a tinny recording of Louis Armstrong's "Melancholy Blues", which happened to be the first song she and Vanderlay had ever danced to.

"Hello," a voice said, "Customer Service. How may I help you?"

"I left a violin in one of your cabs the other day."

"A lot of things get left in our cabs, ma'am. It would be helpful if you could pinpoint which day it was?"

Aria had to think about this. It was unclear how much time had passed. "Um, yesterday, I think, but it could have been the day before."

"Okay ma'am. What is your name?"

The question scratched at her brain. "What do you need my name for?"

"It will be more expedient if I ask the questions, ma'am. Do you have the number of the cab in which you left the cello?"

She thought about the business card she left in the cab's backseat. "Massoud..."

"Massoud Jafari?"

"That's it," Aria said launching into a trot. Pigeons scattered. "Also, it's a violin, not a cello," she added, as she weaved through a group of slowly moving pedestrians.

"I'm sorry ma'am, Massoud Jafari is not working this shift."

She was running now, her aching legs propelling her toward the depot.

"But don't worry," the voice continued, "Massoud is a stand-up fellow, and so if you left an instrument in his cab, it's very likely that he turned it in. Could you please describe any distinguishing features that would make it easy to identify your particular—what was it again?"

Low umbrellas, unavoidable puddles, and this man's annoying interrogation added to Aria's growing sense of frustration. "Look," she said, "did he, or didn't he, turn in a *vi-o-lin*?"

"I am doing my best to determine if that is the case," he said, "but first I have to get all the necessary information"

Aria spotted the yellow sign of the taxi depot at the end of the block. It was then that she noticed how tired she was, not just tired from running, but tired of running, tired of fighting things that she had no control over.

"Okay," she said, "can you just tell me if you have anything that looks like a musical instrument in your lost and found."

"One moment, please."

Aria heard what sounded like a heavy filing cabinet drawer being pulled open.

"Yes, ma'am, we have something that, in my estimation, approximates the size and shape of a vi-o-lin in our lost and found, but as you have failed to answer the necessary questions, I can't be one hundred percent certain that it is in fact your instrument."

"Are you looking at it now?"

"Yes, ma'am."

"Is it in a black hard-shell case?"

There was a muted knocking sound.

"Yes, ma'am."

"Does the case have the name 'Finn and Clay Music' on it?"

"Yes, ma'am."

A feeling of relief swept over her. "Promise me you will not open the case until I get there."

"Until who gets here ma'am? You haven't told me your name."

"Never mind," she said as she stepped through the door.

The small reception area was dark and musty, with panelled walls covered in 1970s baseball pennants and taxidermied fish. When she spotted a frail gentleman dressed in an over-sized suit holding a phone to his ear, she hurried along a well-worn trail in the carpet, past a water cooler and dusty old coffee machine.

"Hi, I'm here for the violin," she said, when she got to his desk.

"Excuse me," he said into the phone. He turned to Aria and smiled. "Funny, I have someone on the line enquiring about a violin, as well."

"What a coincidence," Aria said.

He put the phone back to his ear. "You won't believe this," he said, "but there's—hello?" When he looked back at Aria, he had a perplexed look on his face. "She hung up."

Aria sighed heavily when she spotted the case on the floor. "There," she said, "that's my violin."

He placed it on the desk in front of her. "Always happy when things find their way back home."

She flipped the latches and opened the lid. "Thank god," she said. "You have no idea how precious this instrument is." She picked the violin up and examined it in the light. It really is exquisite, she thought, the grain, the purfling.

"I was wondering," he said, "if someone as passionate about music as yourself has ever heard of the *Golden Record*?"

Aria ran her hand along the neck. When she glanced back at the gentleman rambling on about god knows what, she saw it—the look of someone desperately seeking meaning and hope in the wake of some deep and heartfelt loss.

"It's a recording of the greatest songs ever composed," he was saying. "Part of the Voyager space probe—"

As she placed the violin back in the case and secured the latches, she was reminded of how pain comes in waves and out of nowhere, always catching you unaware—a smell, a memory, an object, and sometimes in the eyes of a stranger.

"Carl Sagan said it was like a bottle in the cosmic ocean, out there in deep space waiting to be discovered."

"Thank you so much," she said, checking the clock. "I'm in a real hurry. Can you call me a cab?"

❧

What felt like tiny feet moving across her body—paws kneading her chest, whiskered snouts burrowing into her pockets—were actually the frantic labours of two women crouched at Bailey's side. She opened her eyes just as the one with sensible white shoes, slipped a cellphone into her purse. “I’ve called an ambulance,” she said. “Just relax and stay put.”

The rows of yellow lights overhead confirmed that she was still under the marquee of the theatre where she had stopped to take shelter from the rain. How she ended up on the ground, she couldn’t remember.

“What’s your name, sweetheart?”

Bailey was just about to answer when she spotted her purse lying on the sidewalk beside her. The latch was undone, and there, among the shifting feet, was a tube of lipstick. And Dhani’s letter. Seeing the envelope exposed and vulnerable on the ground for the second time that day brought her mind into sharp focus. She tried to move, but a hand was placed on her shoulder. When this was reinforced by a second hand, the yellow lights above her began to swirl, and once again, that same feeling of deeply rooted anger bloomed into another explosion of violence.

The woman kneeling at her left took the brunt of the scream in the forehead. Bailey’s imagination added just enough force that the woman toppled into the girl in pumps behind her, who in turn stumbled, and in doing so, managed to hook her fingers in the backpack strap of a seven-year-old boy holding the handle of his mother’s folded umbrella. The woman with the injured foot dragged the kid down on top of her, causing the tip of the umbrella to strike an usher in the groin, who then fell hard against the theatre doors. The matinee inside concluded with a muffled applause.

Bailey grabbed the envelope and hurried past the ambulance pulling up to the curb. I passed out, but I’m okay, she told herself. I haven’t consumed anything but wine, coffee, and an apple fritter in the past two days.

She took out her phone, and there was the picture of the dog that Noah sent. If he had found the dog, she reasoned, then he would have returned it to the shelter. She turned toward the subway and started to run.

❧

Vanya woke up to find Annu still buried in his fortress of blankets. She wanted nothing more than to stay in bed, but there was simply too much to do. She tapped her husband gently on his sheet-covered head. "The sraddha is tomorrow," she said. "You've got twenty-four hours to get this out of your system."

Whatever it was she had experienced in the night now seemed like a dream, and yet she did her best to avoid the reflection in the mirror as she washed her face and hands.

When she was finished with the marjana, Vanya hurried downstairs to the altar where she acknowledged the three murti and then placed a pinch of Panchakajjaya, tilakshata, and gingelly seeds in the puja tray. Touching the sandalwood tilak on her forehead, she then wiped her hands on her apron and headed to the kitchen.

Nine

It was late afternoon when Vanderlay was awoken by the sound of his ringing phone. Rolling to his side, he located his jacket on the floor, reached out and dragged it over to the futon. The call went to voicemail as soon as he answered. The message was from Takeru, a reminder of the world outside of the storm—*I have a table, six chairs, and a couple of Scotch glasses for you. Call me.*

He was about to delete the message, when his phone began to ring again.

"I'm looking for Doctor Stone," the caller said.

"Speaking."

"It's Doctor Holloway, I'm sorry to bother you, but I have a John Doe here. We lost him this morning in the OR. Cardiac Arrest. Type 1 spontaneous myocardial infarction—massive plaque erosion. Anyway, he had no identification, but we did find your business card in his pocket. You're the only contact we have, and so I was wondering if you could come in and ID the body."

Vanderlay rolled onto his back and stared up at the ceiling—a white rectangle of nothingness giving way on all sides to the sharp angles of the empty walls.

"Doctor Stone, are you there?"

The question gave him pause. Here, there, he wasn't sure. He had taken a handful of pills. He had hung up on his wife. And then, in the midst of emergency room chaos, everything had gone black.

He was home, sure enough, but he wasn't sure how he got there. And now he could hear a heavy-metal soundtrack coming from the ceiling. He let the phone fall from his hand, got to his feet, and stumbled toward the stairs. He had to use the railing to pull himself along, and then each step down the hall was an effort unto itself. When he got to the door he didn't hesitate.

Dhani's room was exactly as he had left it, cluttered and yet ordered like a museum exhibit filled with personal artifacts—a pair of slippers neatly placed at the foot of the bed, sheet and blanket pulled military-tight at the corners, a desk, a computer monitor, an electric guitar, an amplifier, a stereo.

As he perused the shelves full of CDs and DVDs, he noticed that the band names all seemed to represent something lethal and foreboding—Venom, Hellhammer, Mayhem, Dark Throne... The video games had equally disturbing titles—*Abomination, The Nemesis Project, Counter Strike, Halo, Call of Duty*, something called *Duke Nukem*.

He was reminded of the day when Dhani asked for a Game Boy Advance. At the time, Vanderlay didn't really know anything about video games, hadn't paid much attention since high school when he and his friends used to feed quarters into the 2D arcade console called *Asteroids*. In his mind, it was all just a harmless waste of time—rudimentary graphics, cheap sound effects. But when Dhani unwrapped the hand-held console on his twelfth birthday, Vanderlay took note of his son's dilated pupils, the increased cardiovascular activity, and the slight hyperventilation that were classically symptomatic of someone who had just ingested an opioid. And indeed, like a drug user, before the batteries even wore out, his son was petitioning for something better. His plea for a PlayStation included a number of promises involving chores and grades. Despite these warning signs, Vanderlay and Aria decided that as long as Dhani kept up his end of the bargain it was a win-win situation. But the PlayStation brought with it the disturbing soundtrack of revving engines, gunfire, and explosions, punctuated by their son's exclamations of frustration and anger. Vanderlay consulted a psychiatrist friend, who said it was probably nothing more than a hormonal phase. But Vanderlay wasn't so sure. They got Dhani to agree to a limited number of hours of play per day, but when he moved on to online gaming, the time restrictions they had set became much harder to enforce. Before they knew it, he was playing with and against other users around the world. It was at this point that he started referring to people with names like GameWizrd, and Destroyer7 as his friends.

What else had he missed? Vanderlay wondered. A moment later he had the closet door open. He stared at the neatly stacked boxes and then began tearing the lids open one by one. By the time he was finished, there was a mess of comics, cards, and stamps all over the floor. He kicked the empty boxes aside and headed over to the bed, where he got down on his knees, lifted the skirt, and peered into the darkness. The sweep of his arm exposed a shoebox and a Victoria's Secret catalogue. He placed the box on the bed and removed the lid. The matchbooks inside surprised him. Hundreds of packs, he guessed, perfectly stacked in neat rows. There was nothing particularly unique about them. Holiday Inn, Niagara Falls, Swiss Chalet, The Hard Rock Cafe... What would compel his son to collect such a thing?

He had just picked up a pack with the Air Canada logo on the cover, when he noticed that the power button on the computer tower under the desk was emitting a dull pulse. He reached for the keyboard and hit the space bar. The hard drive whirred, and the screen sparked to life, revealing a desert landscape, a crashed vehicle smouldering on its side. In the distance there was a mosque with holes blown into its walls, military helicopters swarming on the horizon. Dead soldiers were strewn about the battlefield. At the bottom of the screen protruded the business end of a massive gun with the player's virtual hand gripping the barrel. This is it, Vanderlay thought, the end of the world—entertainment that stimulates basic adrenaline-inducing reactions that desensitize the psyche to the comparative mundane stresses of reality. Once mastery of the virtual battlefield is achieved, the logical progression is to enlist and apply one's skills in the theatre of actual war. While I was burying myself in work, my wife was galavanting across the globe, my daughter was vandalizing herself with tattoos and hair dye, and my son was up here in his room learning to kill.

Vanderlay opened the matchbook in his hand, tore a match away, and struck the red sulphur head against the flint strip. He watched it burn down to his fingers and then let it fall to the floor.

A moment later he was standing in the master bedroom, staring at the indents in the broadloom where the bed once sat.

They were an echo of a time when the room was a sanctuary where he and his wife would close the door on the day, crawl into bed and make plans together. Once upon a time. He put on some clean clothes and gathered a few things from his dresser. He then walked downstairs, unhooked the birdcage from its stand, grabbed his phone, his jacket, and the car keys. Once outside, he called the fire department and then set about notifying the neighbours on either side of the house. His voice was eerily calm, like a military representative delivering repatriation logistics. "There's plenty of time to grab anything that you may deem irreplaceable," he said. "You know, photos, heirlooms, that sort of thing. Just in case the rain doesn't put it out." And with that, he casually adjusted the floral cover on the birdcage and followed the driveway down to the boulevard.

When the firetruck arrived, Vanderlay stood back and watched two men drag a heavy hose through a bed of flowers and then secure it to a hydrant. He turned back to the house and stared at the flames coming out of Dhani's bedroom window. It's the things that we can't bring ourselves to face that end up destroying us, he told himself.

"You have a violin with you, again, I see."

"Yes," Aria replied, "I just picked it up at the—" When she realized that she was hugging the case tightly to her chest, she took a deep breath and placed it on the floor beside her. "I've had a crazy couple of days."

The therapist pulled the blinds and took a seat. "What's been going on?"

"I feel like I've made some important headway, but—" She was trying to locate the moment when it all seemed to fall apart, but as she paused to take stock, she found her mind rewinding a lot further than she anticipated. "Ever since the day the Twin Towers went down, I've had this feeling of uncertainty. Watching them collapse like that—I don't know, it just left me feeling as though something wasn't right—like I couldn't trust my eyes anymore. All the things that made up reality as I knew it were suddenly in question. When Dhani joined the military, it seemed like part of me was expecting it—not that specifically, but something that would confirm that I wasn't really in control of anything. Then one morning he walks into the kitchen, texting on his phone. He goes over to the stove, puts a few pancakes on his plate, and sits across from me. He takes one bite, puts down his fork, and says, 'We're being deployed to an FOB in Sperwan Ghar. I'm shipping out tomorrow.' I remember placing my hand on my husband's shoulder. It was the moment when he, the father, was supposed to stand up and intervene, talk some sense into our son, tie him to the damn chair if he had to, call the authorities and tell them that our son wasn't going anywhere. But when Vanderlay didn't stand up, I felt my deepest fear take over my heart, and before I could stop myself, I leaned across the table and slapped my son across the face." Aria shook her head and wiped her eyes with her sleeve. "I've been living in that regret ever since, trying to create an alternate reality."

The therapist offered the box of tissue, but Aria shook her head and wiped her face with her sleeve.

"I've spent the last year living in the chaos of that regret, trying to manufacture an alternate reality."

The therapist nodded. "Yes, Freud called it, 'the medium of a hallucinatory wishful psychosis'."

Aria looked down at the violin in her lap. "Maybe it's just more wishful thinking," she said, "but I have the feeling that this violin is connected to all this." It struck her then—what was it that the old man at the taxi depot had said? Something about a space probe and a record? She pulled up her sleeve. The words, "Find 7th composition," were barely legible on her arm. And with that she was on her feet. "I know there's more time left," she said, "but I really have to go."

When the receptionist in the SPCA lobby called her name, Bailey just looked at her phone and kept on walking. The second hurdle presented itself in the corridor that led to the kennels, when she saw that Jill's office door was open. Just take a breath, she told herself, and hurry past as quietly as you can. Despite the sound her wet boots made on the tiled floor, she managed to pass undetected, but when Emily, a vet doing her rounds, stepped out of Room C, the toe of Bailey's boot hit the door as it opened.

"Hey," Emily said. "Jill's looking for you."

Bailey nodded and waited for her to move, but Emily stood her ground.

"I think it's urgent."

She had no choice but to take a few steps back, which left her standing in front of Jill's office. A sudden crescendo of barking erupted from one of the kennels. Jill looked up from her computer. "Bailey," she said. "I've been—are you okay? Is that a black eye?"

"I'm fine," she said.

"Well, you don't look fine. Have a seat."

Bailey stepped into the office, but remained standing. She couldn't sit. If she did, she might not be able to get up again.

Jill took a moment to arrange some papers on her desk, and Bailey's eyes came to rest on a pad where Jill had drawn something that looked like a rocket surrounded by stars and hearts.

"Do you know anything about that terrier mix from stall three in Room A?"

Bailey felt the urge to let the whole story out, but the truth was mixed up with unpleasant thoughts of Noah. So, instead, she pretended to give the question some thought. "You mean the one with the black patch on his eye?"

"Yes," Jill said. "He's missing. I've checked with all the other volunteers and staff, and there's no record of adoption. You're the only one I haven't talked to."

Bailey's eyes returned to Jill's drawing. The longer she stared at it, the more it looked like a bomb rather than a rocket—a bomb that would blow-up as soon as she confessed.

"When was the last time you saw him?"

The question concussed in Bailey's head—the last time she had seen the dog was last night in a dream, sitting at the foot of her bed, his outline intermittently silhouetted by the odd lightning strike outside the window. "Don't go," she wanted to say, but then another flash of lightning illuminated the room, and instead of the dog, her brother was sitting there.

Jill had a confused look on her face.

"I'm sorry," Bailey said. "I lost him."

A long high-pitched howl came from a room somewhere down the hall.

Jill gave her a look of deep disappointment. Each passing

second was marked by a slow and steady ticking.

"I tried to call," Bailey added, "but my phone's broken." She dug her phone out of her purse and showed Jill the cracked screen.

"Your passion and care for these animals is appreciated, it really is, but in light of this most recent event, I've come to the conclusion that this job might not be a good fit for you."

"You're firing me?"

"I don't like that word, but plainly speaking, yes."

Bailey looked for something within reach to smash on the floor, but the tears were already running down her cheeks.

She stepped into the corridor. Another door closed behind her.

After washing and drying the dinner dishes, Vanya lit some frankincense, performed her evening rituals, and then collapsed onto the couch. It had been another busy day prepping for the sraddha while at the same time fortifying the house against a potential attack. Doors were locked, and windows were blocked by pieces of furniture. She felt the stresses of the day softening, but the moment she let out a heavy sigh she sensed a presence in the room. The bookcase she had dragged in front of the living room window blocked most of the light. She sat up and waved a hand in the hazy air. The incense smoke swirled into the shape of another hallucination.

"Good evening, madam." The tiger seemed as real as the stains on her apron. "I'm terribly sorry to disturb you," it said, "but I was wondering if I might take up a bit of your time."

Vanya sat up and placed her feet firmly on the carpet, "You have my attention."

"Well, it's just preliminary business, really, a mere formality, so to speak. In fact, you might consider this a courtesy call."

"I think I know what this is about," she said.

"I confess it took a while to track you down. However, when it comes to the nature of the business that has brought us all so far from home, it is never too late."

The idea of a talking tiger, as polite as it may be, was beginning to agitate her. "What exactly do you want?"

"Would you be offended if I offered a bit of advice?"

"I would prefer," she said, "that you get to the point."

"Well, then, let's just say, now that you've been located, the file of your outstanding debt has been forwarded to collections."

Vanya's mind went to the knife block in the kitchen.

"Oh, don't worry, I'm just a messenger. But agents have been dispatched. This curse, delayed as it may be, will be back on track soon enough."

"Well, if that's the case," Vanya said as sternly as she could. "You are not welcome here." She pushed herself up off the couch. "And if you ever step foot in this house again, I will—" She moved toward the apparition, but with each step closer it began to fade back into the swirl of smoke. Vanya let the momentum of her anger carry her across the room, through the hall, and then down the stairs, where she stepped into the laundry room and reached for the light. The bare bulb flickered and illuminated the old wooden cabinet in the corner. She stared at the padlock for a moment and then gave the small brass handle on the door a tug. The hinges on the cupboard rattled, but the door didn't open. She turned to Annu's tool box on the floor under the utility sink and heaved it onto the dryer. She selected a hammer, tested the weight of it against the palm of her hand, and then headed back over to the cupboard. The lock gave with the first swing.

When she pulled the cupboard open, a dust-covered golf bag fell forward and settled against her thigh. She pushed the bag back with the end of the hammer and sharpened her gaze. Even shrouded in darkness it was menacing enough to make her heart pound in her chest. For a second she considered slamming the door closed and hurrying back upstairs. This thing, she told herself, is nothing more than a tool, and though it once failed my father, I have the advantage of knowing that the enemy is coming.

Vanya put the hammer down, brushed aside a mess of cobwebs, and reached into the closet. With renewed conviction, she kicked the cupboard door closed with her foot, rested the barrel of the rifle against her shoulder, and headed up to the kitchen.

Ten

Vanderlay checked the rearview expecting to see a fleet of police cars, ambulances, and firetrucks—the sirens of his anxiety bearing down on him. But the roads were clear, nothing other than the rain-soaked city and the smouldering ashes of his life fading in the distance.

Once he was on the highway, he selected a disc from the console between the two front seats and slid it into the stereo. A few bars into the opening track, the piano's chords softened the edges of the world. He had the sense that he was passing through a transitional portion of his existence that bisected whatever his life was from whatever it was going to be. Both were moving away from and toward something at the same time.

As the music began to build on a repeating phrase, he turned on the windshield wipers and pressed his foot down on the accelerator. The Volvo responded effortlessly. A second or two later he was driving 30 km over the speed limit. Corporate headquarter buildings, hotels, and factory outlets blurred in his peripherals. Just as he was settling in to the anesthetic calm of the music and the open road, something moved in the back seat. His hands reflexively tightened on the steering wheel, tendons taught across his knuckles.

When he forced himself to look into the rearview, instead of the distorted image he was expecting, he saw the birdcage. He reached back and touched it to be sure that it was actually there. The track gave way to the solemn cry of a muted trumpet, and he began to feel the magnitude of what he had done. The whole thing seemed like a dream. Was he dreaming now, or was he finally awake? Keep driving, he told himself. Don't look back.

The road before him suddenly seemed like something full of possibility, like an open cage door. He tuned his mind to the moment. As Miles began to riff on a scale, Vanderlay was inspired to improvise himself. He turned on the GPS and set the destination to Walden.

An hour later he was crossing the border into Buffalo, which formalized his commitment to the journey. The I-90 took him south along the edge of the city where it merged with Highway I-90 and then curved sharply to the East past the airport. Once he was well beyond the approaching and departing planes, he turned off the stereo, rolled down the window, and let the wind clear his head.

Just outside of Rochester the clouds began to thin, and a glimmer of light appeared on the horizon. After two days of rain he was pleased to see that he had managed to outrun the weather. When the automated voice of the GPS announced an approaching exit, his eyes went back to the sky. Somewhere overhead, he thought, a satellite orbiting the earth is giving me directions. He drove for a spell thinking of the days when road trips were planned out on a map, plotting the journey town by town. Was this just another example of how the things we own begin to own us, he wondered.

When the bird whistled in the backseat, Vanderlay began looking for a place to pull over. He spotted a roadside corn shed, signalled, and pulled onto the shoulder. Turning off the ignition, he started emptying his pockets, was shocked to see that everything he had left in the world fit on the passenger seat beside him—a wallet, a cellphone, a passport, and a book. He turned on the interior light, picked up the paperback, opened it to a random page.

I do not speak to those who are well employed, in whatever circumstances, and they know whether they are well employed or not—but mainly to the mass of men who are discontented, and idly complaining of the hardness of their lot or of the times, when they might improve them... I also have in my mind that seemingly wealthy but most terribly impoverished class of all, who have accumulated dross, but know not how to use it, or get rid of it, and thus have forged their own golden or silver fetters.

HD had said that there was more than one kind of prison, and Thoreau seemed to be saying that the accumulation of dross is one of them. Vanderlay looked back at Dolittle.

As he climbed out of the driver's seat, the speed and proximity of the passing cars made the world seem volatile and dangerous. He placed the cage on the gravel, turned to the oncoming traffic and put out his thumb. A long spell passed, during which he did his best to keep his mind focussed on the journey. Everything behind him was destroyed. All he could do was use the force to propel him forward.

The chill in the air was just beginning to seep into his bones when an SUV pulled onto the shoulder ahead. He picked up the birdcage and made his way to the idling vehicle.

"Car trouble?" the driver asked.

"You might say that."

"Where are you headed?"

"Boston."

"I can take you as far as Springfield."

As he waited for the driver to gather a pile of garbage from the passenger seat, he felt his anxiety give way to a rush of excitement—as soon as they were off, somebody else would have their foot on the accelerator, their hands on the wheel. "I appreciate this," Vanderlay said as he climbed in.

"No problem," the driver responded, "I need all the karma I can get." He took a sip from a travel mug and then returned it to the cup holder. "I noticed your plates are Canadian," he said as he put the vehicle in gear.

"Yeah," Vanderlay said. He placed the cage down on the floor between his feet. "I'm a big Red Sox fan. I drive down to a game every now and then." He didn't like lying, but it was so much easier than trying to explain that he was seeking solace in the philosophies of a hobo he had met in jail.

"What's with the bird?" the driver said, pulling onto the road.

Before he was even sure how he was going to respond, Vanderlay found himself telling the driver that he had a lot of money riding on the game and that Dolittle was his good luck charm. The driver laughed and took another sip from his travel mug.

It didn't take long before Vanderlay exhausted whatever knowledge he had about sports, and the conversation faded.

"Grab that CD there, will you?" the driver asked.

Vanderlay reached forward and pushed a pile of coffee cups, pop cans, and chocolate bar wrappers aside. "Madonna, or *Russian for Beginners*?"

"That's it," the driver said. "The Russian one."

He slipped the disc into the stereo. "I met this lady on the internet, and well, there's a bit of a language barrier."

"*Kak pazhivayesh?—How are you?*" the voice on the CD said.

The driver repeated the Russian phrase out loud, a subtle slur in the rising inflection at the end of the sentence.

Vanderlay turned toward the window. They were passing farmhouses now, crops of corn and soy.

"Spaseeba preekrasna!—Fine thanks!"

He stared out at the dark line of trees on the horizon and then up at what was now a clear star-filled sky.

"Gavareetye pazhalooysta myedleeney—Could you please speak more slowly?"

As the driver's hesitant responses grew more emphatic, Vanderlay realized that there was more than just coffee in his mug. Christ, he thought, what have I got myself into now?

"Yah khachoo paprobavat' natseeanal'naye blyoodo—I want to try some national dish".

He was just about to ask the driver to pull over when his phone rang. The moment he saw that it was his daughter calling, he felt something spark in his chest, the strike of flint on stone.

"Bailey?"

"Dad—"

"Aseetreenoo pa rooskee—poached sturgeon with tomato sauce and vegetables."

"Yes, sweetheart. I can't hear you too well, the signal is bad."

"Are you at wor—"

"No. I'm actually not sure where I am. I'm, well, on the road."

"I want—" her voice broke up again, "come ho—"

Vanderlay looked down at his phone. No, no, no. "Bailey?"

"I can't hear—" Her voice deteriorated into an intermittent signal of syllables and silence. And then nothing.

"Schyot pazhaloosta—Bring the bill, please."

Vanderlay rolled down the window. The things we rely on most, he thought, fail us when it matters most.

He watched through the side mirror as the phone skipped and bounced on the asphalt until it disappeared.

❧

When Bailey placed the phone she had borrowed on the counter, Barb, the SPCA receptionist, looked up from the computer monitor. “Is everything okay?” she asked. “That didn’t sound like it went so well.”

“I think my father just hung up on me,” Bailey said.

Barb picked up the phone and replaced it with a box of tissue. “You are really having a bad day,” she said. “Losing a dog, breaking your phone.”

“And I was fired.”

Barb gave Bailey a sad look, and then stepped out from behind the counter.

For a horrifying moment, Bailey thought she was going to give her a hug. “Have you seen Noah around?” she asked by way of distraction.

Barb strolled past her. “He hasn’t been in all day. I was just about to make a coffee. You want one?”

The mention of a coffee reminded Bailey that the cafe where she had lost the dog was just down the street. It was a long shot, but what if the dog had returned to the scene of the crime, as it were. She grabbed a handful of tissue and hurried out the door.

The girl at the counter had a dirty cloth in her hand, the bangles on her wrist clinking as she wiped down the espresso machine. “We’re just closing,” she said when Bailey walked in.

“I wanted to say I’m sorry,” Bailey offered as she approached the counter.

The girl gave her a perplexed look.

“Yesterday—You spilled coffee on me. I freaked out. Smashed a mug before I left.”

The girl shrugged. “Coffee gets spilled and mugs get broken all the time around here.” She moved over to the sink and started rinsing the cloth. When she looked up again she seemed surprised to see that Bailey was still there.

“If you want anything,” she pointed at the self-serve carafes, “it will have to be to go.”

Bailey grabbed a large paper cup. “I’m looking for a dog.”

"We don't allow dogs in here, so—" She reached over the counter and grabbed the cartons of cream and milk.

"I lost him outside on the corner," Bailey said, as she selected something called Morning Glory. "He's a terrier mix with a patch on his eye."

"A patch on his eye," the girl said turning from the fridge, "what, like a pirate?"

"Not an actual patch—his fur colour—" Bailey took a sip of the tepid coffee. "I thought he might have come back here. Maybe you've seen him hanging around outside?"

"Nope," the girl said. She stepped out from behind the counter, strolled across the floor to the door and flipped the sign. "The coffee is on the house. I was going to throw it out anyway."

Bailey stood her ground, "Can I at least leave a poster on your notice board?"

"We open tomorrow at 7 am," the girl said. "But right now, we're closed."

Bailey felt the tears coming again.

"Really," the girl said, "I have to be somewhere."

It was then that Bailey knew that her position in the world had finally become utterly and completely invalid.

When she let the cup drop to the floor, the girl smiled. "If I was your dog," she said, "I would have run away too."

After pulling the police tape down, Aria entered her apartment, went over to the fuse panel, flipped the breaker, then turned on the overhead light. A moment later she was wandering through the maze of furniture and boxes searching for her laptop.

She carried it over to the stool in the kitchen and hit the power button. Dhani's image filled the screen. The photo captured a portion of his outstretched arm, his head tilted away from the lens of his cellphone. His face was sunburnt and tired, his smiling eyes shadowed by his combat helmet. There was a bullet-pocked wall behind him. Even though seeing her son in military uniform made her heart ache, she had set the picture as her screensaver. It was the last photo he had sent her. She forced herself to stare at it a moment longer and then clicked on the browser icon. A window opened, and his face was obliterated.

Despite having done this a million times, she typed the titles of the six compositions into the search field and scrolled through the results. After several pages of concert listings, videos, and Wiki entries, a familiar feeling of frustration began to take over. This is hopeless, she thought. But then as she blinked at the screen, something caught her eye at the bottom of the page. She dragged the cursor down to a heading called "Murmurs of Earth: the Voyager Interstellar Record." Where had she heard that before? She opened Oliver Silverman's website and scanned the Links: *The Mutual UFO Network, The Aetherius Society, The Aerial Phenomena Enquiry Network*, and—*NASA Voyager Probes.* The NASA link took her to a page called "Mission Overview". Another click and there on the navigation bar was *The Golden Record.* She scrolled over it, and a drop-down menu appeared. *The Golden Record* was a recording NASA had placed on the Voyager probe back in 1977, in case the probe encountered intelligent life out there in deep space. The record contained images, greetings, sounds, and—when she clicked on the "Music" icon she was taken to a list of compositions—"Oh my god," she whispered.

Vincent had no idea what he had seen on the hospital roof. The wind, rain, the lights, and his own anxiety made it impossible to be sure of anything. He had stayed awake all night trying to work up the courage to call the police, the CIA, or whatever authorities deal with unidentified chaotic disturbances in the sky, but they would think he had lost his mind. He just couldn't bring himself to make the call. When the grey light of morning had filled his bedroom, he worked up the nerve to make an anonymous call to the hospital, informing them that a patient had been seen on the roof. While this eased a part of his mind, he still didn't know what to do about the violin. Over a breakfast of toast and tea, he considered his options: he could either check himself into a psychiatric facility, or he could toss a brick through the window of Finn and Clay, vandalize a few cash and carry items, and report the violin stolen. In the end he chose to do what he always did—go to work and act like everything was fine.

He got through the day by keeping himself busy restocking cable displays, capos, picks, tuners, guitar straps. He reorganized the sheet music, dusted the amplifiers, and tuned every guitar in the shop. At 6 pm he locked the door and sat himself down at the Bosendorfer. He was half-heartedly muddling through a Hoagy Carmichael tune when he heard a tap on the front window. As he hesitantly approached the door, he could see a pair of bloodshot eyes peering through the foggy glass. He reminded himself that the neighbourhood had always been full of colourful characters and that his assumptions about people had been wrong on several occasions. He had heard virtuosity in the hands of greasy-haired rock guitarists, bluegrass banjo players, and once in the abilities of a scruffy kid who tied an emaciated Rottweiler to a bike rack, strolled into the shop, and picked up an accordion. He was just about to unlock the door, when he remembered that letting someone in the shop after hours had led to the ill-fated lending of the Boulangeot. Be kind, he told himself, but do not let him in. When the door was open enough to talk through, he placed the toe of his shoe securely against the frame. "Can I help you?" he asked.

"Yeah, this is a music store, right?"

Vincent's eyes went back and forth from the shopping cart to the dark red stain on the front of the guy's shirt, "Yes," he said, "like the sign says—Finn and Clay Music."

The guy stepped back, grabbed the handle of the shopping cart, and swung it around in front of the door.

"Woah," Vincent said, "you can't bring that in here. And—" he pointed a finger at the sign, "—we're closed."

"Okay, okay, can you at least tell me what this is?"

Vincent opened the door a little more and leaned out for a closer look. "Recycling?"

"Wait," the guy whispered, and started pulling the bags of beer bottles, tin cans, and plastic out of the cart.

Vincent was about to push the door closed, when he saw something metallic catch the light.

"There," the guy said. He stood back as if he had just unearthed a buried treasure. "It plays music sometimes—"

Vincent leaned in closer. There was something reminiscent of an instrument in its chrome, brass, and copper tubes and valves, but he hadn't seen anything like it before. "What is it?" he asked.

"That's what I'm asking you."

They both stood there staring silently at the wonder of it.

“It looks like the result of a high-speed collision between an orchestral brass section and a glockenspiel.”

“How much do you think it’s worth?” the guy said.

Vincent felt strangely compelled to reach out and touch it. “I really couldn’t say.”

“This thing is a one-of-a-kind. I bet it’s worth as much as one of those pianos.”

Vincent shook his head. “I can’t help you,” he said. But as soon as the guy started loading the bags back into the cart, he felt the urgent need to stop him from leaving. “You said it plays music?”

“Yeah, sometimes, like it’s picking up some kind of a signal.”

“What kind of music?”

“All kinds of stuff. Classical, rock and roll, and some weird stuff too. One song had, what do you call it, panpipes, and one song sounded African.”

“Probably some kind of radio,” Vincent said.

When he pushed the door closed, the guy stuck his own shoe in the way.

“Wait,” he said, “it’s doing it again.”

The music was quiet, but Vincent recognized it immediately. Mozart, *Queen of the Night* aria, which reminded him of the violin, the very thing he was doing his best to not think about. “Maybe it’s a cappuccino machine,” he offered. “There’s a Starbucks down the street. See what they say.”

Vanya had the rifle slung over her shoulder as she maneuvered the vacuum through the living room, the dining area, and up the stairs to the bedrooms. She carried it as she hauled a load of laundry up from the basement, and she had it with her as she continued her preparations for the sraddha. By the end of the day, the house was in order. With a pot of sweet porridge and a larger pot of dhal simmering on the stove, she turned on the radio.

She was wiping at the flour dust on her apron when the news report mentioned that one of the escaped tigers had been run over and killed. A hesitant smile cracked the thin line of her lips, but the relief she felt was tempered by the fact that a second tiger was still at large. The singularity of the threat meant her surveillance had to be that much more keen. She turned off the radio and made her way to the living room window. The rain was falling hard, blown about by random gusts of heavy wind. Poor visibility. As she scanned the neighbourhood, her eyes came to rest on the recycling bin sitting at the foot of her driveway. The fact that she had forgotten to retrieve it was one more example of how tired she was.

When she got to the front hall, she unslung the rifle and leaned it against the wall. There was a relief from the release of its weight, but she didn't feel comfortable the moment it was out of reach. She quickly slipped her feet into her boots, slid her arms into a coat, and pulled the door open. The heavy rain gave her pause. Suddenly every bush, hedge, and tree had become potential cover for a stalking predator. She looked back at the rifle and then out at the dark street. Just get it over with, she told herself.

She kept her eyes locked on the bin sitting at the curb, as she hurried down the walk-way. The moment she had her hands on it, she turned and pulled it back up to the house. Once it was parked next to the gate, she ran back to the door, pushed it closed, and stood there breathing in and out, the thick and heavy worry of her inherited fear.

Eleven

By the time the driver hit the breaks, it was too late. The deer thudded across the hood and then slammed into the windshield. The SUV went into a skid and came to rest facing the opposite direction it had been travelling in.

"Christ," the driver said, "not again." He put the vehicle in park and looked over at Vanderlay. "You okay?"

"Etee tooflee zhmoot—These shoes are tight."

Vanderlay pulled the cage up onto his lap. The bird was standing in a wet mess of newspaper and seed. It wasn't until Dolittle chirped that Vanderlay nodded. "It looks like we're fine."

The driver ejected the CD, then sat there for a moment staring at the steering wheel. "I think the left-front tire blew," he said. "I already have two priors, and I don't have a spare. We need to call a tow truck and tell them you were driving."

"That's not a good idea," Vanderlay said. "I'm in a bit of trouble myself."

The driver looked at him for a second and then reached for the mug that was now on the floor by his feet. "All right," he said, "I guess I'll have to report the vehicle stolen." He pushed the door open and then looked back at Vanderlay, "You're bleeding."

Vanderlay flipped down the sun-visor mirror. There was a cut over his left eye, probably deep enough for stitches. He pressed his sleeve against the wound and watched the driver staggering off into the dark. I need to get the vehicle off the road, he told himself, and then slid over to the driver's seat. Once the SUV was on the shoulder, he stepped out into the night air, took a deep breath, and followed the skid marks that led back to the deer lying in the road.

The doe's belly had split open, exposing its intestines and stomach. Vanderlay reflexively began his assessment. Time of death—approximately midnight. Cause of death—impact with a speeding vehicle. What could be gleaned from this collision, he wondered. The simple reasoning that *bad things happen—wrong place at the wrong time*—just wouldn't do. There were so many circumstances, coincidences, and decisions that lead to the intersections we arrive at each day. He knew it was pointless to concern himself with the countless subtleties of each and every calamity, and yet, this death was proof that every decision we make is connected to every decision everybody else makes. If he hadn't been hitchhiking, this deer would have arrived at this place several minutes after the SUV went by. If he hadn't driven his son to the airport—

He took a hoof in each hand and pulled the carcass toward the ditch, wondering if the deer had any offspring of its own, lives that would now be unequivocally turned upside down. His mind went to the hospital, where an emergency call paged over the loudspeakers activates a team of advanced care providers. Nurses, anesthesiologists, and doctors sprint through the halls. But out here in the real world, he thought, you're alone, with cars careening down highways, marriages falling apart, and improvised exploding devices blowing lives to smithereens.

Once he got the animal off the road, he felt strangely compelled to lay down in the ditch next to it, but then he remembered the bird, the book, and his destination. He turned once again to whatever it was that might lay ahead, and started moving toward it.

❧

Bailey stood outside of the coffee shop staring down the street where the dog had disappeared. She knew it was time to give up. This is it, she thought, there's nothing left to do but go back to my apartment and wait for the landlord to come and kick me out.

She started walking, head down, miserable, but before she made it to the end of the block she was frantically checking her purse. A quick search confirmed that she had run out the door that morning without her keys, which meant that she had no way of getting back into her apartment. She felt the colour draining from everything. The storefronts, the traffic lights, everything had become as grey as the sky. Getting out of the rain seemed like the only thing that mattered.

She arrived at the subway station feeling like an apparition with no purpose, lost between worlds. She shuffled through the turnstiles and let the dismal weight of her soaked clothes pull her down the stairs. As soon as she arrived on the platform, two lights appeared in the darkness of the tunnel. A moment later, the blast of a train entered the station, the squealing brakes, the chime of opening doors. She took a seat, pulled her hoodie up tight around her face, and leaned her head against the window.

The train surged through the tunnel. Her eyes half-closed and blurred with tears, Bailey's mind drifted to a long-forgotten weekend—fireworks on the lake, the last of the cascading colours fading, her father raising his arm and pointing. "There's the Big Dipper. See those six bright stars..." At the time she was astonished by the realization that there was some kind of recognizable order up there. But then, as he guided her eye to a number of other constellations, she saw that he was systematically transforming a billion wish-fulfilling dots of magical light into something scientific and nameable. A crack had formed in her heart that evening, and though she was too young at the time to know it, she had resented her father ever since. She could see now that the obliteration of that innocent wonder and mystery was inevitable, and that it was her father's rational way of looking at everything that she now needed—to hear him explain away all the crazy shit that had been playing tricks on her mind.

When the automated voice announced the station closest to her father's home, she got up and dragged herself over to the doors. Her wet feet sloshed in her boots as she climbed the stairs, and headed back out into the rain.

She passed the familiar landmarks of the neighbourhood—the primary school, the rec centre, the park where she had her first kiss. Nothing registered, nothing but more shades of grey.

Bailey knew that a hot shower, a meal, and warm bed wouldn't change how messed up her life was, and yet, when the boulevard of the house came into view, her spirits lifted. But then she saw the tire tracks on the lawn, the grass now a rutted mess of sod and muck. A few more steps and she was at the foot of the driveway, staring at the plywood covering the front door, the black scorch marks on the brick outside the upstairs windows, the charred and partially collapsed roof. She turned to the street, searching for someone who might explain what had happened, but there was nothing but streetlights and shadows, homes with their curtains drawn, a quiet and familiar indifference.

❧

After leaving Finn and Clay Music, the guy pushing the shopping cart made his way over to Yonge Street to try his luck at the pawn shops. By the time he got to end of the block, he was beginning to feel like he would never find anyone interested in the contraption in the cart. The manager at Buster's Buy and Sell pretty much summed it up. "We don't buy or trade equipment, gear, or apparatus that can't be categorized. It's got to be a musical instrument, or an appliance, or plumbing hardware, or a piece of sporting equipment, or a medieval torture device, or whatever, as long as it's got a name. You get the idea? I don't know, what the heck that thing is, and you don't know either. Until one of us does, there's no way I can determine its value."

A guy at the recycling centre offered him its scrap price by weight, provided he pull it apart and separate all the different types of metal into the appropriate containers. He turned down the offer, but he took the $34.80 he got for the plastic and glass bottles, which he used to purchase $8.00 worth of scratch cards and a small tube of Anbesol toothache gel.

Once he had a pocket full of change, he decided it would be more expedient to locate a buyer by phone. His search for a booth with a working phone and a phonebook took him to the top of Spadina Avenue. He first looked up "Restaurant Equipment", but as he eyed the machine through the dirty glass, he confirmed that, despite a few vague similarities, it really didn't look like it could produce an espresso. The heading "Salvage" turned up a handful of options, but the nearest place was somewhere out in the deepest part of the suburbs. "Scientific Instruments" looked promising, but when he discovered that several of the pages in this section of the phonebook had been torn out, he kicked the door, which swung open and hit the shopping cart. A moment later it was rattling down the incline of the street. Without a thought he went after it, the change in his pocket jingling, his jawbone pounding as he ran. When it became clear that he would not reach the cart before it got to the intersection at the foot of the block, he cut through a used car lot and disappeared into the night. The shopping cart spun off onto the boulevard, skipped over the curb, tipped onto its side, and skidded to a halt under a streetlight. The machine emitted an almost imperceptible plume of vapour, which would have gone unnoticed if it weren't for the SPCA employee extracting a mangy raccoon from a sewer grate a few metres away.

Noah placed the cage he was carrying into the back of the van and strolled over to the machine. He gave it a nudge with the toe of his wet shoe. Whatever it is, it sustained some damage, he thought. One of its copper tubes had a dent in it, and a shiny cylindrical plate had come away from a brass globe housing some kind of a gyroscopic device that was now spinning freely.

A pair of headlights appeared at the top of the hill. Getting the contraption off the road seemed like the obvious thing to do, so he carried it to the van and slid it into the back with the cages.

Five minutes later he was driving along River Valley Road. He parked under the yellow haze of a street light and sat there for a moment, scratching at the scabby tattoo on his shoulder. The collective distress of the caged animals filled the vehicle. Mixed with the faint sound of violins from the machine in the back and the steady rhythm of the wipers, it made a solemn soundtrack to his thoughts. He looked at himself in the rearview and then nodded, as if he had just made up his mind about something he'd been mulling over all day.

As he carried a cage holding a raccoon across the field, he scanned the path that ran along the river for potential witnesses, but there was no sign of activity anywhere. He put his cargo down by the trees and repeated this routine until all twenty-six cages were lined up in the wet grass.

This is it, he thought as he opened the first cage door. I'm actually doing this. But instead of the mad rush to freedom he anticipated, the overweight tabby inside hesitated, as if it could sense the danger waiting in the dark. It wasn't until he gave the cage a little kick that it stuck its head out and ran for the trees. The rabbits needed to be prodded with a stick before they hopped out into the rain. Likewise, the iguana wouldn't move until he gave the cage a shake. The raccoon poked its nose out, but then retreated. Noah raised the back end so that it slid toward the opening and then scurried off into the bushes. And so it went until each and every cage was empty. "You're all better off," he said. "Free of the whims and infatuations of teenage girls."

It was then that he realized a guy walking a pair of overweight pugs was watching him from the shelter of a large willow tree, pointing a cellphone at him. Noah ran.

As he made his getaway, his anxious driving was made that much more erratic by the feeling that he was being followed. He took a series of quick and random turns, ran a yellow light, made an illegal left, and then pulled into an alley. Sitting there, listening to the sound of his racing heart, he began to wonder if the thing he had been trying to outrun was actually in the vehicle with him. He turned and looked, expecting to find a forgotten cage, but the only thing there was the strange contraption he'd found on the road. A moment later he had the back doors open. "One more stray," he said. He carried the machine over to a blue dumpster, heaved it up onto the edge, and gave it a push.

When Vanya went to check on her husband, she found him with the blankets still covering his head. This has been going on long enough, she thought. She went around to his side of the bed, leaned the rifle against the side table, and pulled the covers back. To her surprise, his face was bloodless and gaunt, his eyes vacant. "Oh, my God," she whispered. She placed her hand on his forehead, then hurried to the bathroom and she dampened a cloth under the tap. "Annu," she whispered as she placed the cool cloth across his forehead, "you're burning with fever."

She spent the next three hours at his side, checking his temperature, and replacing the cloth when needed. When he finally nodded off, her eyes drifted around the room. Everything seemed to be cloaked in a shroud of neglect and decay. Even the rifle leaning against the table suddenly looked ancient—the finish on the wood, dull and thin, the metal tarnished. It was in this hazy lull that she realized just how much faith she had been placing in a weapon she knew next to nothing about. She reached for the rifle, looked back at Annu to make sure he was still sleeping, and then headed to the spare room.

She almost fell asleep while she waited for the old computer to start up, but once the search began, a renewed sense of conviction kicked in. A half hour later she was on a website that identified her father's rifle as an Enfield Mk II. From there, she found several videos documenting the history of its service, how to dismantle and clean it, and, most importantly, how to fire it.

She gathered some cleaning supplies and dragged Annu's tool box up to the bedroom. She proceeded to check the rear sites, inspect the bore, and lubricate the bolt and trigger, all the while whispering softly to each part she handled. She was rubbing lemon oil into the wooden stalk when she found herself imagining her father, the leather strap of the Enfield secured over the rough wool shoulder of his warden jacket. She had always pictured him as a handsome man with a kind face, tall and thin, a man who might have difficulty finding a shirt that fit him in the sleeves, a man who was, as her mother insisted, incapable of taking care of himself long enough to fulfill his fatherly duty. He, like so many before him, didn't believe in the curse until it was too late. "In some ways," her mother had said, "it makes perfect sense. Men barge around with their big ideas, but they are children at bottom. They need supervision. Otherwise they go traipsing off into the world and blunder into the path of a predatory animal."

Vanya placed the rag on her knee, raised the rifle to her shoulder, and drew a bead on the clock. Without thinking, she pulled the trigger. The bolt snapped forward with a hard satisfying click. She was imaging the power of such a thing actually firing, when it dawned on her that the rifle was not loaded. This revelation struck her as yet another trick of the curse—something to be checked and corrected immediately.

She made her way downstairs, imagining the spectre of the tiger, saliva dripping from its jowls as it chuckled in the shadows. When she got to the basement, she shoved the laundry room door open and went straight to the cupboard, reached into the cobwebby darkness and dragged her hands across the shelves. Nothing. She hurried back up the stairs and checked the closets, the cabinets, and the cupboards under the kitchen sink. She checked the buffet and hutch, the drawers in the end tables, and then headed upstairs to search each room on the second floor as well. By the time she gave up, there were open boxes and odds and ends on the floor in front of every closet in the house. There isn't a tree in the world that Lord Rama hasn't shaken, she told herself. She spent the next hour praying in a cloud of burning sandalwood.

Aria laid there in bed staring at the exposed ductwork on the ceiling. Her mind was racing with excitement and apprehension. Discovering that the music was from a recording placed on a deep space probe was making her reconsider the possibility that the music she'd heard in the Registan Desert might be an actual alien transmission. But what would it matter now that the machine was gone. Her mind spiralled toward the same conclusion that nothing really mattered now that her son was dead. Maybe the sraddha will help, she thought. But then she was reminded of her parents and—"When did it start?" she asked out loud. The question led all the way back to the first violin she had ever played—music class, grade four. When she brought the violin home, she went to the basement and sat on the cold cement floor. She opened the case and examined the instrument's contours, its structure, the hollow woodiness of it. She placed it in her lap and started plucking the strings over the bridge. When she got a sense of the tone of each string, she used her other hand to press down on the corresponding strings along the neck. Each resonating note seemed to suggest which note should be played next. Before long she was experimenting with tempo and rhythm. At some point it began to feel like the instrument and her own body were vibrating together, like they were connected. But then her mother appeared at the foot of the stairs with an armful of laundry. She ushered Aria into the living room where her father was sitting and reading the newspaper, catching up on what he called, "the state of the world's karmic debt."

"The gods have blessed our daughter," her mother said. She then perched herself on the arm of the couch and tilted the lampshade so

Aria was cast in a warm yellow light. “Play,” she commanded.

But Aria didn’t think of it as playing. In fact, it was something else entirely. She stood there in a state of inert defiance until the timer beeped in the kitchen and her mother went to tend to whatever was in the oven. When she looked at her father, his attention was back on the newspaper. Without the scrutiny of an audience, Aria sat down with the violin in her lap and began to search once again for the part of herself that bonded with the instrument. And once again, her explorations resulted in a harmonically textured melody.

When she stopped playing, her father folded the newspaper, got up from his chair and gestured for her to stand. Aria got to her feet, and he held out his hands. “May I?”

She watched him quickly tune the instrument and then tuck it under his chin.

“Like this,” he said. “First position.”

He drew the bow lightly across a string, lifting it after the stroke. “Colle.”

He handed the violin back to her, but when she held the instrument as her father instructed, it felt painfully awkward.

“Go ahead,” he said.

She drew the bow, but the violin only howled and whined.

Her father made a small adjustment to her bow arm and nodded. “Again. This time elegant and graceful.”

She tried again. It still sounded like she was torturing an small animal.

“Lower the elbow,” he said.

The violin quivered and wailed.

Her father’s voice was louder this time. “Keep the bow parallel to the bridge.”

The same anguished response.

“Frog to tip. Full bow. One stroke, one beat,” he said, this time guiding the speed and tension of her arm.

When she intentionally drew the bow in a reckless manner across the strings, he shook his finger. “Aria. Behave.”

She pulled the violin to her chest, one hand gripping the body, the other wrapped around the neck.

“First position,” he said again.

Aria shook her head. “It hurts,” she said.

Her father directed her to pull the violin in tighter to her chest. His voice got louder. She heard the tailpiece creak. And still she held on with all her might. When she felt something snap, she dropped the violin and ran to her room.

Her father came home later that evening with a brand new instrument. "I'm sorry," he said. "That violin was no good anyway. We'll start fresh in the morning."

He took her on as a student with the same fervour that her mother applied to the daily rituals of their culture. Practice began right after morning prayer at 7 am. They started with exercises to develop finger dexterity, and then he introduced her to the positions along the neck. From there she moved on to string crossings, bowing patterns, and articulations.

While other kids were watching television and playing in the park after school, Aria was memorizing passages from the Vedas and bowing three-octave scales, arpeggios, and broken thirds. By the time she was in high school, his regimen of practice and her mother's cultural etiquettes had become so strict that she missed parties, pop culture references, sporting events, crushes, all the things that she overheard other students talking about in the halls.

On the one occasion that she complained, her father looked at her and said, "This is difficult music. And if you let it into your heart, you will know that it is, like our religion, the remedy to all the pain and suffering in the world."

Aria got out of bed and picked up her phone. It didn't matter what time it was. Something had to be done.

Twelve

Vanderlay approached the Blue Moon Motel looking like a man who had survived a night in the wilderness, a man in need of sleep, food, and shelter. But the thought of a soft bed just reminded him that he had recently lit his house on fire, abandoned his car on the side of the highway, and thrown away everything he had. There would be no bed, no pillow, no roof to shelter him. He was on foot in uncharted territory, moving toward what ever might come. He turned instead into the gas station, the fluorescent lit aisles of snack food, its takeaway conveniences.

A trail of dirt followed him into the store and marked each step down the aisle. He tried to focus on the things that he needed not the things that he wanted: a loaf of bread, a jar of peanut butter, a bottle of water, a toothbrush. When he got to the counter, the clerk smiled uneasily and started to ring in each item. Vanderlay pointed at a selection of backpacks hanging above a display of pencils, markers, pads, and binders. "I'll take one of those, as well," he said.

"Skip Hop Zoo, Hello Kitty, or The Little Mermaid?"

Vanderlay paused. "Doesn't matter—"

"I might have a Ninja Turtles pack in the back. Is it for a boy or a girl? "

"It's for me."

"You might find something in adult sizes at Costco in Albany, but they don't open until 9 am."

Vanderlay nodded as if he was giving this some careful consideration. "The one with the cat is fine."

As the clerk went over to the display and grabbed the Hello Kitty pack off the rack, Vanderlay's eyes went to the clock. 3 am. No wonder I'm exhausted, he thought.

"Anything else?" the clerk asked as he scanned the barcode on the pack.

"Not unless you happen have some bird seed."

"We've got sunflower seeds on the rack there behind you. Otherwise, you'd have to go to Costco in Albany."

Vanderlay grabbed a pack, tossed it on the counter, then looked out the window. The black asphalt of the parking lot was orangey yellow under the streetlights. Beyond that he couldn't see much more than forest on the other side of the highway "I don't suppose you know if there are any train tracks nearby going east?"

"There's some track about a half-mile up the road, but the closest station is in—" the clerk's voice tapered off, "—Albany."

Vanderlay took out a credit card. As he waited for the transaction to go through, he tore open the pack of sunflower seeds and poured some into the cage.

"I know it's none of my business," the clerk said, "but you should probably have that cut on your head looked at."

Vanderlay tucked the credit card back into his wallet and started loading his supplies. "I'll have it looked at when I get to Albany," he said.

When he stepped outside, the lights behind him cast a thin raggedy shadow across the parking lot. Limping, stooped, and leaning to the left. A pack in one hand, a birdcage in the other. "This is it," he said to Dolittle, "Can't say how this is going to turn out, but we are dross free."

The ringing that woke Annu up sounded like a distant alarm, some kind of a call to action. He pushed the covers down, climbed out of bed, and shuffled slowly to the door. By the time he made it downstairs to the kitchen and reached the phone, the caller had hung up. He stood there a moment then went to the sink. Thirsty, he thought, turning on the tap. But then he couldn't seem to make sense of what came next. He reached for the cutlery drawer. It opened halfway and jammed. The knives, forks, and spoons gave him pause. Had he wandered into someone else's house? When he turned to the table he recognized the plates, the glasses, the bowls, the business of it all, but now he couldn't recall why he'd gotten out of bed, why he was standing in the kitchen in the dark.

He was back out in the hall when the phone rang again. He looked up the stairs and then back at the kitchen. He had been sleeping. And now the phone was ringing. Answer it. That made sense. Answer the phone to find out what he must do next.

"Hello?"

"Hello, Mata ji?"

His daughter's voice was strangely hesitant and vulnerable sounding. He guessed that something must be terribly wrong. He turned to the hall and called out to his wife, but his voice disappeared in the dark halfway up the stairs. When he found his way back, the phone cord was spiralled around his waist. "Your mother is sleeping," he said. "I guess you're stuck with me."

He heard Aria's breath catch.

"I'm sorry for calling so late," she said.

"That's okay," he responded. His mind pawed in the dark for something meaningful to add. "Your mother's been busy. The kitchen is a mess."

"I can imagine," she said. "She's taking the whole sraddha thing very seriously."

"Yes, the sraddha," Annu repeated. It struck him then that something had indeed gone wrong. The gods were angry.

"Papa—"

Her voice was brighter now.

"Yes?"

"I started playing again."

"Playing?"

"The violin."

The mention of the violin had him stumbling. The word was tangled up in so many things: pain, joy, the failure of his own two hands. "I'm glad," he said. "It broke my heart when you stopped—"

"I know," she said.

"The truth is, I wanted you to succeed where I had failed."

"I'm sorry for letting you down. I really am."

His head was beginning to clear, and he could now recognize what the conversation was about. "You never should have had to bear such a loss. It was supposed to be me."

"I'm sorry for that too. We've each been messed up by it differently, but it's all equally messy and unbearable."

A moment passed where neither of them spoke, and in that pause his eyes fell on the weather station on the wall.

"It's good to hear you're playing again," he said. "The rain has stopped, and the humidex is returning to normal."

"Yes," she said, "I think the storm is finally over."

It took Bailey a second or two to realize where she was. The darkness and the dense fog obscured the details of the world around her. When she shifted her weight, a pool of water gathered in the tarp spilled onto the patio. She got up from the Costa Rican hammock she was lying on, shoving the memory of her burned-down house back into the grey fog around her. She stumbled across the lawn, squatted next to a neglected bed of petunias, and had a pee. This is it, she told herself, my first day as a homeless person.

She left the property feeling inconsequential, without a sense of purpose or direction. There was a lightness in her body now that confirmed that her transformation into a persona non grata was almost complete. When she emerged from the residential area onto Yonge Street, the fog-shrouded lights and the closed storefronts made the world seem even more desolate and lonely. She wandered aimlessly, slogging through puddles, ignoring the lights at intersections.

The rain eventually got so bad again that it drove her into a 24-hour drugstore. Inside, she stumbled past a security guard, through a cacophony of fragrances, and into a blaze of brightly lit aisles. Deodorant, she thought as she passed a display of bubble bath. And a toothbrush. Before long she was heading to the checkout with her arms full. As she waited for the cashier to scan each item, Bailey found herself staring blankly at a rack of magazines and newspapers. Celebrity faces and headlines blurred in and out of focus.

"$84.60," the cashier said.

It took a second for Bailey to realize the clerk was speaking to her. "I'll pay with Visa," she said as she opened her purse. She inserted the card into the machine, keyed in her PIN, and then drifted back to the magazine rack. Somewhere in that stupor she heard the word, "Declined." Bailey rubbed at an itchy eye and got the cashier to remove the honey-vanilla lip balm and the Claritan, and turned once again to the rack of magazines and newspapers. Royal wedding scandals, celebrity pregnancies and divorces, and then—*SPCA Employee Releases Animals in Don Valley.* In the photo, Noah was captured luring a pair of guinea pigs out of a cage with a handful of grass.

"It's still not going through."

Bailey placed her hand over her mouth. When she screamed, no one in the store seemed to notice.

The first thing Vanya noticed when she woke up was that the room was unusually dark and silent. She listened for Annu's raspy breath and then reached over to his side of the bed. When her hand fell on the empty space, she shoved the covers aside and got up.

She checked the bathroom first, headed out into the hall, called out, and then rushed downstairs. The chair jammed against the back door confirmed that if he had left the house he'd done so out the front door. The tiger, she reasoned, as suave as it was, could have persuaded Annu to unlock the deadbolt. She hurried to the kitchen and pulled open the cutlery drawer, but it jammed as it always did, so she had to reach blindly past the utensil tray to grab the flashlight.

Her mind was racing through a number of horrible scenarios when she got to the front hall. As she reached for the door, something moved in the shadows to her right. She dropped the flashlight, its beam resting to illuminate a mess of shoes, a pair of galoshes, a single rubber boot, and two bare heels. A moment passed before she realized that she was pointing the barrel of the rifle at the dim shape of her husband, who was on his toes searching the shelf above the coat rack.

"I need a ladder," Annu said.

Vanya turned on the hall light, and Annu stepped out of the closet blinking at the brightness. "What are you doing with a rifle?"

"I was worried," she said, slinging the strap over her shoulder. "I thought something terrible had happened to you." She pulled him toward her and placed her hand on his forehead. The fever was gone. "What in the world are you doing in the closet?"

"I was looking for my violin," he said.

It was such a relief to know that his self-imposed exile was over, and that, despite being up in the middle of the night, he seemed relatively cogent. "It's 5 am," she said. "The sun's not even up yet."

"The barometer is a little low," he replied, "but the conditions are otherwise optimal."

Vanya took him by the hand and led him down the hall. By the time they got to the stairs he was rambling on about temperature, air pressure, and mass flow. She smiled and nodded as she coaxed him up each step.

When she finally got him back into bed, she kissed him tenderly on the forehead and climbed under the covers beside him. "The violin is in your bottom drawer," she whispered as she turned out the light.

365 days after Dhani's death

You are untethered. Adrift. You watch the things that might save you pass by, but you do not reach out. To be rescued would mean you have given up on your pain. It would mean that you have accepted the loss, failed once again to care deeply enough. And so you continue to flounder, going under and then resurfacing, nothing and then pain, over and over again. It would be easier, you think, to give in, to simply allow this thing to swallow you, to be washed into the stomach of it, to be tumbled and roiled into a petrified state, a living husk. But a damned part of you continues to hope. As you rise and fall, you know there is light somewhere. There once was, and so there must be. All you can do is open your eyes, take another breath and look to the horizon, just over the tallest wave, and move toward the spot where one grey thing meets another.

Thirteen

On the one-year anniversary of his son's death, Dr. Vanderlay Stone found himself watching the sunrise through the open door of a slow-moving boxcar. The factories he was passing—yards littered with splintered rail ties, broken lawn chairs, and discarded tires—seemed to mirror the state of his weary mind. He leaned back against the hard wooden side of the car and let his mind drift, Before long the cadence and rhythm of the train had him thinking of depression-era images, guitar-playing hobos, wheat fields and crows, a tin cup and a can of beans. Just as he was drifting off, the train slowed, the whistle blew, and Dhani appeared in the frame of the open boxcar door. Vanderlay was aware that the shadows and distortion usually involved in these hallucinations were absent—no mirrors, reflections, or compromised light. And yet, there he was.

"Sorry," Dhani said, "I didn't realize this car was occupied."

Vanderlay pushed back against the urge to get up and give him a hug.

"Is that a budgie?"

"Yeah," he answered hesitantly. "It's Dolittle."

"What are doing on a train with a bird?"

Vanderlay could see that he had lost weight and that his hair was different, somewhere between its usual length and the cut of a soldier. "I'm on what you might call a pilgrimage," he said.

"A pilgrimage, what, like to a holy temple or something?"

"Are you familiar with the work of Henry David Thoreau?"

"You're taking your bird to Walden?"

It was clear now that the eyes were different, and the tone of his voice was a register lower too.

Vanderlay felt deep disappointment. "I am."

The kid, whoever he was, smiled at him. "I hate to be the one to break it to you, but Walden is really no big deal. I mean, it's not worth planning your holidays around. And anyway, you're on the wrong train."

Vanderlay moved toward the door and stood there, trying to process his two most recent errors.

"You need to get back to Albany. Catch a train heading to East Boston."

When he turned around, the kid was pointing a cellphone at him.

"You mind if I take your photo?" he asked, "I've never met a real hobo before, at least not one that was lost."

Bailey watched the dark sky lighten to its usual dull grey from the window of a Tim Horton's. When they eventually kicked her out, she spent an hour down at the harbour sharing the sandwich that she had bought with a pile of seagulls. She eventually wandered into the city's main square, where she stopped under a banner advertising an interactive basketball festival. The latest hip-hop hits were being blasted over the heads of a huge crowd gathered around a bunch of makeshift courts, where kids of every ethnicity were engaged in a series of three-on-three contests. She couldn't think of anything worse than having to make her way through such a large crowd, but when she turned around, the street behind her was filling up as well. As she paused to consider her options, she noticed that there, just beyond her reflection in the tinted glass of the building next to her, was a radio-station studio where a sixty-ish bald guy with stylish, thick-rimmed glasses was waving her in. Astonished by the fact that he could see her, Bailey waved back and then wove her way to the buildings entrance. Once inside, the DJ signalled for her to take a seat in a chair that seemed expressly positioned for guest-spot interviews. At a commercial break, he removed his headphones, reached over the console, and shook Bailey's hand. "You look lost," he said.

A million thoughts skipped through Bailey's head. It seemed vital to get it right, to give voice to the incoherent, tangled mess of her life, and yet, the first thing out of her mouth involved the runaway dog.

It turned out the DJ was an animal lover. He handed her a Kleenex and asked what breed it was.

"He's a mutt," she said, "some kind of a terrier mix with a patch on his eye."

"—like the dog on the RCA record label?"

Bailey nodded.

"Is there a number where you can be reached?" the DJ asked.

"Yes, if anyone has seen him please call me at—" The tears started again.

The DJ took a bite out of what looked like a baloney sandwich. "Are you okay?"

"I don't know," she said. "The world is so messed up, you know. I got fired, my parent's house burnt down, and..." Bailey inhaled deeply. "Oh my god."

"What is it?" the DJ said.

"What day is it? Is it Sunday?"

"It is."

Bailey was on her feet. "I have to get to my grandparents' house right away."

In her panic, she banged into a microphone stand, tripped on a cord, and almost went through the glass wall. The momentum of her breakdown carried her out the door and into the crowd, and then her broken cellphone started to ring.

As Vanya snored away, Annu laid there, staring at the dark ceiling, listening to the memory of morning traffic—two-stroke motorbikes, dogs barking, the distant sound of a crowing rooster. These sounds were soon accompanied by images of coloured fabrics and the smell of jasmine and sandalwood. He wasn't sure if this homesickness was real—whether he was awake or dreaming—but he felt energized in a way he hadn't felt in years.

He took a quick shower, brushed his teeth, trimmed his moustache, and then headed back into the bedroom. He slid his arms through the sleeves of a clean white shirt, put on his trousers, knotted a tie, and grabbed his suit jacket. Then he went to the bottom drawer of his dresser, pulled it open, and removed the violin.

In the kitchen he made toast, and since his wife's cooking had left no room at the table, he stood at the counter as he ate. He was dabbing at the corners of his mouth with his tie, when a sheet of paper stuck to the fridge caught his eye—test results from the doctor's office. Something about early onset cognitive impairment. He folded it into the shape of an airplane and tweaked the wings before checking the design from several angles. Once he was satisfied, he picked up the case, tiptoed past the stairs, and headed for the door.

When he got to the sidewalk he launched the paper plane. It spiralled for a moment in the damp air, before it caught a breeze and headed westward, rising steadily as it wove its way around the tall oaks that lined the boulevard. Annu followed.

Vanya woke up to find Annu's side of the bed was empty again. She laid there wondering what mischief he might be getting himself into. If he's well enough to get up and get dressed, she thought, it means that he might be well enough to help with the sraddha. All he needs to do is follow the instructions I've written out, and this whole affair around Dhani's soul can be laid to rest. The gods will be appeased, and Annu and Vanderlay will be made safe again.

She was on her way to the bathroom when she saw that the bottom drawer of his dresser was open. Her heart began to race. A moment later she was heading down the stairs with the rifle.

Fourteen

Vanderlay had been hiking for two hours when he came to a service station. He inquired about the town of Albany, and the guy manning the fuel pump said it was another fourteen miles away. Vanderlay stared off at the long stretch of road ahead and then headed over to the phone booth. He knew calling a cab was a cop-out, but he was too exhausted to continue on foot, and he didn't feel comfortable hitch-hiking again.

After making the call he found himself thinking about something Takeru once told him about a guy in Japan who had installed a phone booth in his garden so that people could contact loved ones that had passed away. What would I say to Dhani, he wondered. It struck him then that whatever regrets he had, and whatever apologies he might make, should be addressed to his wife and daughter. He stared off at a nearby cornfield swaying gently in the breeze, the sky a deep and fathomless blue. He felt the pull of it. Onwards.

He hung up the phone and then hobbled over to a stretch of grass, where he opened the backpack, dropped a handful of seeds into the cage, and settled back with the book.

Each page that he read turned in his mind with equal parts wonder and curiosity. What stands before us unnoticed and what passes far beyond seemed to intertwine in Thoreau's stream-of-consciousness ruminations on undisturbed solitudes and stillness, the pleasure and value of contemplation, the many things that may be learned through observation, the simple rewards of time spent using the senses, that no exertion of the legs is required to bring together two hearts and minds. It is all, he seemed to be saying, here and now, not in what has been done or may be done, but in the thing we are doing.

When the cab arrived, Vanderlay tossed the book in the pack, and grabbed the cage. The driver rolled down his window. "I need to see some money before I let you in," he said.

Vanderlay was about to protest, then he saw his reflection in the cab's window. The birdcage in his hand, the cut on his forehead, the dried blood. He took out his wallet and showed the driver a fifty and three twenty-dollar bills.

"What's that?" the driver said.

"What's what?"

"That's no good to me."

It took him a second to realize the driver was rejecting the Canadian currency.

"Add the exchange rate to the fare," Vanderlay said. "Any bank will convert it for you."

The driver put the car in gear, "I don't think so," he replied.

"I'll pay you double."

The driver gave this a moment's thought. "Double and an extra twenty for the bird," he countered. "I'm not supposed to allow animals in the cab."

Vanderlay reached for the door and then paused. Whatever system that had once determined the transactions in his life was suddenly gone just because of the way he looked. "Never mind," he said, "I think I'd rather walk."

Three hours later, Vanderlay was standing in front of a six-foot-high fence between the road and the rail yard. With the cage balanced in the hook of his thumb, he jammed the toe of his shoe into a link and hauled himself up. When he swung his leg over the top, he felt the cuff of his pants snag, which left his crotch precariously balanced over a row of twisted wire. After some maneuvering he managed to free his leg and reach until the cage was about a foot from the ground on the other side. He let it drop. Dolittle fluttered in the air then jumped again when Vanderlay came down hard on the ground, leaving a swatch of his trousers hanging from a knot of wire at the top of the fence. He could feel a trickle of blood running down his thigh as he turned toward the trains.

When he spotted one pulling out of the yard in an easterly direction, he grabbed the birdcage and started to run.

❧

As the streetcar approached the stop, Aria was thinking of the conversation she'd had with her father the night before and how it had softened the pain in her heart and the sharper edges of world around her.

Clutching the Boulengeot tightly to her chest, she climbed aboard, took a seat, and turned to the window. She couldn't remember the last time she had gotten up so late in the day or had awoken from such a deep and dreamless sleep. She felt something close to what she once called normal—a mixture of uncertain feelings to be sure, but no longer the relentless feeling of worry.

As the streetcar came to a stop in front of a coffee shop, the scent of roasting beans, notes of toast, burnt sugar, and chocolate reminded her of the day she met Vanderlay for the very first time— he was wearing a worn wool sweater, a textbook of some kind open in front of him. Handsome, earnest, and swarthy. When he caught her staring, he held her gaze until she turned away. The next time she looked up from the journal she was writing in, he was standing at her table. "I know this is really forward of me, but I was wondering if I could take you out to dinner. Tonight," he'd said. "If you happen to be free." The next thing she knew she was giving him her name, number, and address.

When he picked her up, he handed her a single yellow rose, and then opened the passenger side door of his car. The perfunctory conversation was pleasant, but she found the music he had on to be discordant and loud. Without giving it much thought she reached for the volume on the stereo, "Jazz can be so annoying sometimes," she said. "I don't know what's so special about flattening notes, or swinging quavers with a dotted rhythm."

"Jazz is a pure expression of improvisation and virtuosity," he said, "and Thelonious Monk is one of the greatest pianists to ever live. That recording you just interrupted is as noteworthy as any by the world's foremost composers of classical music.

Aria didn't hesitate. "To compare," she said, picking up the CD sitting on the console, "*Straight, No Chaser* to, say, Bach's

Goldberg Variations, is superbly obtuse. But the issue is, I found the music distracting."

Disappointed at how quickly things had gone sideways, she opened the window and turned her face toward the din of the street. She was thinking about telling him to let her out at the next red light when to her surprise he apologized.

"I was out of line," he said, "I'd like it if we could start over."

When he smiled at her, she felt herself soften. "Deal," she said.

Things got complicated once again at the restaurant, when he ordered a sweet and rich Zinfandel while she chose an oaked Chardonnay. But then he surprised her again. "Differences," he said, "are learning opportunities. Just as jazz and classical are both complicated forms of music with their own particular merits, the preference of white and red wine does not negate a shared appreciation of viticulture." As the evening played out, an after-dinner conversation revealed that they were both impressed by the risotto and how exquisitely the crème brûlée paired with the twelve-year-old Courvoisier. By the end of the night she had made up her mind. He was articulate, ambitious, handsome, an atheist, and most importantly, didn't know an allegro from a legato. She imagined that marrying this man would be an act of emancipation, a way of escaping her parents' strident influence—their absurd notions regarding religion, culture, and the transcendent virtues of Bach.

As the streetcar approached her stop, she saw the sraddha as chance to recognize differences as learning opportunities, to confront the wounds that have torn her family apart, to start over.

Bailey placed her free hand over her ear to block out the noise of the crowd and aimed herself at the tall buildings on the other side of the square.

"Hi," the voice said. "I heard you're looking for a lost dog."

"Yes," she answered, "have you seen him?"

"I have. In fact, he's here with me now."

Bailey stopped in her tracks. "Is he all right?"

"Well, I suppose that depends on how you look at it."

The crowd around her hummed with activity. "What do you mean, how you look at it?"

There was a pause on the other end followed by the sound of a dog barking. She started moving again, twisting and turning through a sea of elbows and shoulders.

"He's in pretty rough shape," the caller said, "but he's not in any pain."

As Bailey continued to blindly push through the crowd, she lost all sense of direction.

"Sit," the voice said. "Sorry, he's pretty excited."

"Where are you?" she asked. "I want to come see him."

"Sorry again," he answered, "you can't come and see him, that would be impossible."

The low battery prompt flashed on the screen of her phone, and Bailey's movements became more aggressive. "Please, just tell me where you are."

"Bailey?"

"What?"

"I want you to know that there's no need to worry. He's fine now, out of harm's way."

There was something about those words that gave her pause. When she stopped, the crowd closed in around her. Instead of the panic she expected, she felt strangely calm. She became part of the rising and sinking swell of bodies, instead of being swallowed, let herself be carried across the square and then released into the middle of a small pavilion of kiosks—tie-dye shirts, djembes, hemp handbags, beeswax candles, burning incense.

"Bailey, are you still there?"

She turned toward her grandparents' house. "I'm on my way," she said. She didn't wait for a reply, nor did she expect one. The line was dead.

❧

With the violin swinging at his side, Annu followed the paper plane to the end of the block, where a breeze pushed it north up an intersecting street. With each step, he felt a vitality returning to his body. Not only were the variables in the earth's atmosphere ideal—temperature, density, and pressure were uniquely stable, but the forces that were now guiding him were free of worry or uncertainty. He had the feeling that his whole life had been leading to this moment, to this intersection, to this performance.

When Vanya got to the front door and saw that the deadbolt was unlocked, the panic in her chest thickened. Her impulse was to rush out the door in her housecoat, but then she remembered that the rifle she was carrying was not loaded. She made her way back into the living room and knelt in front of the altar. Don't think, she told herself, the work has been done. She closed her eyes. Now it's time to listen.

Annu whistled, and the paper plane descended in a long slow curve around a cherry tree and then headed off west on Danforth Avenue. He followed it to the lights and then north across the intersection, where it circled a few times around a lamp post before disappearing through the doors of the subway station.

In the concourse, he spotted the plane gliding past a woman with a stroller who had just opened the gate between the turnstiles. He slipped through after her, closed the latch behind him, and followed the plane down the stairs. The moment he arrived on the landing, it came to rest on the floor in front of a closed newspaper kiosk. There were escalators and more stairs at either end of the passage way leading down to the trains. "Just in time for the morning rush hour," he said.

As the voice of Vanya's worry slowly gave way to a quiet calm, the room filled with the vague shapes of multi-armed deities, some with serene faces, others with tongues and teeth exposed. When the prayer was complete, she remained on her knees waiting for a response. The moment she opened her eyes, she turned from the shrine and headed for the kitchen. When she saw the cutlery drawer, all the mystery was gone from it. "Destruction, it is," she whispered. She tightened her housecoat and then pulled the drawer open.

Annu tightened the hairs on the bow and then drew it across a piece of rosin. Once this was done he ran a cloth along the neck of the violin, tucked it under his chin, and gave it the requisite tuning. The next few minutes were spent warming up with a slow arpeggio and a double-stop exercise, concentrating on attacks, releases, and tone. Once he felt limber enough, he closed his eyes and began with a piece called "Invitation to the Dance". The opening moderato allowed him to find a comfortable tempo, his fingers softening to the remembrance of play and precision. He could feel his blood begin to flow, his head becoming clearer, the rhythm returning to his knees and hips. By the time he approached the allegro vivace, he was back in the old train station in Kurnool.

After maneuvering the drawer past the spot where it always stuck, Vanya pulled the whole thing out and placed it on the counter. The space behind the cutlery tray was filled with odds and ends that had remained out of sight for years—wooden spoons, napkins, a cheese grater—and there at the very back, under a takeaway menu, she found the clip of rifle shells. A moment later she had the butt of the rifle resting on her thigh. She pulled the bolt up and then straight back as far as it would go. Then she pushed the clip down hard with her thumb and advanced the bolt, which stripped a bullet from the magazine and slid it into the chamber.

As the East and West trains arrived, the morning rush-hour traffic flowed up the escalators and converged in the hall in front of Annu. The commuters, though set on getting to the waiting buses at the top of the stairs, slowed as they passed. With each step the chaotic movement of the crowd seemed to align itself into a collective rhythm. As Annu attacked the final vivace of the third movement, the small corridor in the train station felt like a place of worship, its ductwork ceiling and tiled walls transformed into marble, burnished mahogany, and gold leaf, with deities of hope and redemption descending.

Fifteen

Low skirts of pinewood were slowly panning by as Vanderlay got himself up and leaned out the door of the boxcar. There in the distance he spotted a flock of crows resting on a sign. As the train got closer, the words, "Walden Pond State Reservation," came into focus. He quickly put on the backpack, grabbed the bird cage, and returned to the door. The train was moving slowly enough, but still much faster than he would have liked. There was no other choice. He slid his legs over the side of the car, then heaved himself off the edge.

While he did his best to keep the birdcage upright, when he came to rest, the trough of water was empty, the ladder had disconnected from the side, and the sunflower seeds were gone. "So sorry," he said wiping the dirt off his pants, "I'm clearly not cut out for this hobo stuff." He got to his feet and headed over to the road that led to the park entrance.

Just inside the gate he came to a bronze statue. The sign next to it stated that Walden Pond drew more than six hundred thousand annual visitors. Boating, fishing, swimming, hiking, baptizing opportunities, and of course, its allure as a pilgrimage destination, brought people to its shores from far and wide.

At a glance, there really wasn't much to it—a visitor's centre, washrooms, and a short path that led to a ten-by-ten log cabin. Vanderlay strolled across the parking lot, waited for a group of tourists crowding out of the narrow door, and then stepped inside. A fireplace at the far wall was flanked by a table and chair on one side, a wooden kindling box and a bed on the other. This can't be right, he thought. The building had the look and feel of something recently made. He concluded that the cabin was a replica and turned back to the door.

In the parking lot, a group of teenagers were lifting some kayaks off a trailer. He followed them down a walkway that led to the beach. At the far end, he came to a trailhead lined on both sides by a low fence to keep people from venturing into the bush. As he entered the forest, the cheerful warble of birds that greeted him was underscored by the distant whistle from a train somewhere beyond the oaks and white pines.

Aria walked in the front door of her parents' house expecting to hear Vanderlay, Bailey, and her parents in the kitchen, but everything was silent. She called out as she kicked off her shoes, and then again at the foot of the stairs leading up to the second floor. Still nothing. Maybe I got the date wrong, she thought, heading into the kitchen. The air was thick with the smell of spices: fenugreek, cumin, cardamom, cinnamon, and sandalwood. As usual, her mother had overdone it. The table was covered in bowls and plates that coloured the room with a nostalgic sadness. So many conversations, painful, joyous, and regrettable, had taken place here. It wasn't hard to picture her mother working over the stove, her father returning home from work, placing a box of gulab jamun and cham cham on the counter. "Quickly, my little prodigy," he would say, as he picked Aria up and held her in the air, "grab Lakshmi's owl by the tail." Aria followed the memory as it circled the kitchen table, and then flew through the door leading to the basement.

By the time she got to the bottom of the stairs she felt like she was nine years old again. This is where it all began, she thought. She took a seat on the cold floor, opened the case, and raised the violin to position. She drew the bow across a string. The sound was a far cry short of the harmonic standards of her father. She lowered the instrument onto her lap, then started again, this time focussing on the space between the notes, the silence that gave each phrase meaning—each pause, stop, rest, and breath as integral as each note played.

Beethoven's "Cavatina" slipped almost seamlessly into the first movement of the *Brandenburg Concerto.* As the resistance in her body softened, she remembered something her father once told her—" The goal is to play until you are no longer playing, to transcend the limitations of your ability, the instrument, and the music itself. It is here that beauty, faith, and love converge, and we find ourselves, exquisitely in tune with the gods."

She moved effortlessly into the *Prelude of the Well-Tempered Clavier*, and then into the Stravinsky's *Rite of Spring*. By the time she got to the seventh composition, Aria was playing with an unrestrained passion and fervour. She felt something akin to what her father had promised her, but then, as soon as she began the final passage of the *Partita*, the ever-present ache in her chest began to once again colour her performance, and she felt a familiar feeling of frustration and anger surge through her veins. But this time, when she felt the full impact of the loss that shattered her heart, she kept playing.

She didn't encounter God, or anything thing else resembling an answer. In fact, all she could feel was the presence of her pain, or no: she now noticed something else there too, something that hadn't been there before.

"I'm so sorry," she whispered.

When she opened her eyes, she was cradling the violin gently in her arms.

Leaves swirled and gathered in Bailey's wake, as she made her way to her grandparents' house. The world seemed vaguely alive with energy and wonder—a seatless bicycle chained to a tree, an abandoned umbrella—everything seemed illuminated. When she looked up at the sky, the grey was giving way to a feint tinge of blue that seemed to spread and brighten toward the horizon. Something began to ease in her, like a fist unclenching. She stopped, leaned herself against the window of a barber shop, pulled out the envelope, and broke the seal.

> Dear Bailey,
>
> There's a tradition that dates back to Hellenistic battles, when soldiers used to write farewell letters to their loved ones before

going to war. According to my C.O. these letters are no longer standard procedure, but they are recommended. I tried to think of it like an operations report, a documentation of objectives, damages, and outcomes, but every time I'd start the damn letter my mind would wander and I'd find myself remembering things that now seem so much more meaningful than they did when I experienced them. This morning I found myself thinking about a time when I was about fourteen—I don't know what was going on with me, but while I ate breakfast I pulled the petals off one of the roses Mom had brought in from the garden. Later in the bathroom, I crushed the toothpaste tube in my fist. And then when we went to Nani and Nana's house. While you were all out in the backyard admiring Nana's garden, I wandered into the living room. I was fascinated by that shrine, and as I stood there staring at those little brass statues I found myself thinking about how Nani believed that our lives are governed by the cycle of samsara, how we could come back as a bird, and—before I could stop myself—I reached out and snapped the three sticks of incense. As soon as I did it, I felt as if I had done something unforgivable. I started looking for some new incense to replace the ones I broke. I checked all the living room cabinets and every cupboard and drawer in the kitchen. Behind the cutlery tray, in a mess of twist ties and elastic bands, I found a clip of rifle shells. I took one of the bullets from the clip and held it in my hand. I felt excited and terrified at the same time. I had never encountered a thing that was designed to destroy like that. Anyway, I was reminded of the cosmic function of Shiva. That destruction is a part of the supreme trinity.

All those years later, when Dad questioned my decision to enlist, I told him that joining the military was a practical decision. The benefits were great, the pay wasn't bad, and it was an organization with plenty of room for advancement. I closed my argument with some malarky about the opportunity to travel and experience the world, but what I really wanted was to fire a C7 assault rifle.

I have to admit I didn't really know what I was getting myself into until the training started: the seventeen hour days, the obstacle courses, swimming and treading water, thirteen-kilometre marches in full combat gear. Just when I was thinking I couldn't take it anymore, they had each of us dig a hole five feet deep, and then made us live in it for three days. The blisters on my hands were the worst part at first, but then the dampness and isolation began to seep into my bones, and I couldn't stop thinking about how much I missed you all. On the first night, as I lay there on the cold earth, I realized what a horrible mistake I had made. I spent several hours thinking about ways I could get discharged—I heard someone once shot themselves in the knee—But then, at about four in the morning I had a profound experience. It was as if my soul disconnected from my body. It was frightening to be untethered like that, but then I realized that I was looking down at myself sitting in a grave I had dug with my own two hands. I freaked out, but then I began to relax into the idea that some part of me was actually dying. At the end of the third day I crawled out of that hole feeling as if I was reborn, like a part of me had been freed from the confines of my corporeal body. I know this all sounds really strange, but I had the same feeling yesterday when I saw an Afghan eagle. As I watched it soar into the distance, I felt my soul go with it. And as it flew across the desert, I had the sense that it wasn't coming back.

I guess what I'm trying to say is that if you are reading this, then in a way I never really climbed out of that grave, and well, if I am dead, if I'm truly dead, I want you to remember me and carry me with you as a reminder that the only thing worse than the fear of dying, is the fear of living.

TTFN,

Dhani

After waiting to let a city waste vehicle pull into the alley in front of her, Vanya tightened her grip on the rifle and made her way toward the entrance of the subway station. The moment she stepped inside, a group of teenagers looked up from their phones and hurried out of her way. A crowd emerging from the stairs in the fare zone, turned when they saw her, and scurried to the exits that led out to the bus bays. When she got to the fare booth, she leaned the rifle up against the counter. "How much for a senior?" she asked.

"$2.00," the attendant said, backing away from the window.

Vanya opened her wallet and started counting the change. "All I have is $1.85."

The attendant had retreated to the far corner of the booth. "That's fine," he said.

"That's very kind of you," Vanya answered as she dumped the change into the receptacle. She grabbed her purse and the rifle and headed toward the stairs.

Struck as they were by the virtuosity of Annu's performance, the two transit constables doing their rounds were unaware of the anxiety and panic on the platform below until a crowd of commuters came rushing up the escalators. There was no time to get out of the way, so they stood their ground and bore the rush like two rocks in a flood. When the crowd was gone, they were left in a strange calm, except for Annu, who was still somehow, deeply and obliviously, immersed in his playing.

A disturbing sound drew their attention back to the platform exit at the end of the corridor. One of the constables reached for his baton, while the other opted for the pepper spray. For a moment, the soundtrack of the violin made the anticipation of the thing the crowd had been running from, seem all at once surreal, beautiful, and exquisitely terrifying.

When it appeared at the top of the stairs, it did not disappoint. There was no mistaking its beauty or its purpose—piercing yellow eyes, head low, padded feet silent on the cool concrete floor. Its tail swayed gracefully in time with the pauses and attacks of Annu's performance.

Aria put the violin case down on the coffee table and turned to the shrine in her parents' living room—Ganesha, Kali, and Nirhita. As she got down on her knees, she was aware that these gods had always been a part of her life. Even when she told herself that they were nothing more than characters in a pantheon of absurd stories, she had felt their presence. There are things that, whether we believe in them or not, are true, her mother had said. She turned her mind to the transmigration of her dead son's soul, and lit the incense.

The moment the constable with the pepper spray realized that she was standing between a tiger and the music that was attracting it, she panicked and engaged the nozzle far too early. The repellent exhausted itself in a thin mist several feet short of its target. She backed away slowly until her heels came down on the toes of her partner's shoes, a collision that snapped him out of his fear-induced paralysis. On their way up the stairs, they sprinted past Vanya, who stopped on the last step, dropped her purse, and calmly invoked the power of shiva.

The trail eventually led to a clearing, at the centre of which were nine three-foot-high pillars that marked the original location of Thoreau's cabin. Other than the stone foundation of the fireplace, there was nothing left, but the cabin being gone, Vanderlay realized, was of little consequence. Thoreau had come here to live deliberately, to confront the essential facts of life, to see if he could learn what they had to teach. Vanderlay turned to the trees, the broken rays of light illuminating sections of the ground, leaves, rocks, fallen branches, and the path that led down to the pond.

It was clear to Vanya that the tiger making its way toward her husband was more powerful and terrifying than all the manifestations she had battled in her mind. Not only was it much larger, but its predatory eyes cast a spell that made it feel like her own eyes were open under water. It took her several seconds before she managed to push through the trick of the tiger's gaze, but when she did, her actions were fluid and natural. She released the safety, positioned the rifle against her shoulder, exhaled, and drew a bead on the curse that had plagued her family for generations. Annu struck the final note of the "Chaconne", the cat pounced, and Vanya pulled the trigger.

The note, resonating in perfect pitch with the gunshot, echoed through the corridor, rose up the stairs, passed through the atrium, and kept on going. Annu stood there with his eyes closed and his arms extended, listening as it rode a southerly breeze down the alley where it settled over the city waste-management vehicle sliding its forks into the dumpster's sleeves. There, as the cogs and gears of the machine began to turn, the curse, and all the garbage surrounding it, tumbled into the refuse hopper, where it was unceremoniously crushed by the hydraulic compressor.

Vanderlay carried the cage down the slope that led to the water's edge. From where he was standing, the pond looked as it may have all those years ago when Thoreau stood in the same spot. Here,

Vanderlay told himself, is where the past and present and the future converge. He placed the cage on the ground and squatted next to it. "You do your best to protect your kids," he said. "You feed them, shelter them, shed light on a conundrum or two, but at some point they inevitably venture forth on their own. Despite your efforts, there's no way to get through it without failing them."

When he opened the cage door, his body began to tremble. His pulse quickened. His blood vessels distended. His lacrimal glands swelled. As the first tear rolled down his cheek, Vanderlay Stone felt bird-boned, light enough to take to the sky.

Acknowledgements

Thank you to John Vigna, Michael Redhill, Jeff Honsinger, Bob Young, Jeremy Luke Hill, Kasia Jaronczyk, and Lisa McLean for their feedback along the way, to The Common cafe, and to the Creative Writing MFA program at the University of Guelph.

About the Author